The Princess And Her Defender

By

Donna Luers Webster

Weave* Star Productions

weavestarproductions@yahoo.com

USA, 2006

ISBN 978-0-6151-6554-7

Dedicated to my heroes:

Donald L. Luers, Sr., Richard P. Webster &
Jesus Christ

The Princess and Her Defender

ONE

red cord

She was cold. Each shallow breath of dank-molded air shivered its way through her body. Teasing her limbs with the promise of oxygen, the air, stained with the stench of weeping blood and worm -worn flesh, mocked the spark of life within her. She was wounded deeply but the pain harnessed all of her body so that she could barely remember which part of her had yielded to it first.

It was dark; deepest, starless dark. She could not see the filth-caked, threadbare tatters that clothed her. She lay still upon the soft dust that carpeted the hard, stone-floored cell .She was too weak to move her hand and it had long since numbed to all sense of touch. She would die soon. This, she ken'd. She would die soon, alone and cold; her last breath would be full of pain and etched in utter misery. This, she ken'd also. Tears ran dry upon her cheeks. Her eyes were sore. No ag remained to bathe them. They were closed. It did not matter. All was so dark with eyes opened or closed. Her soul was numb beyond despair. She lay still, quietly counting the fading beats of her beater.

It was so black, this time-long night. It was so deeply dark. Nothingness echoed around her threatening to absorb her in its vacuum. The darkness would eat her away, soon... very soon. There was nothing she could do.

She lay still, shivering; quietly counting the whispering beats of her beater.

A tiny wish winged its way from the depths of her soul; one last thought. A last wish before she surrendered what little remained.

"If only my eyes could see light ---just a bit of light--- before they stare unseeing----before they crumble into the dust on which I lay...."

"One-----two------four-----------no, three---------her arms ached; never would they hold a child--------one-----------two-----------three--------was it all for nothing, then? ---------four.

So dark................"

He was prepared. For what seemed like eons, he had equipped himself for this moment- and beyond. He had never met her; but, he had pledged himself to her safety, to her well-being.

Enton, equipped for battle with his Golden Shield in hand and his double-edged sword in scabbard at his side; he burst into the clearing at the top of Nunatok. The rush of his arrival carried on before him and ruffled her garments, as if a wind had disturbed the pristine air of this quiet place.

So this was she... the Gossamer Child. It was she whom he was to deliver, whole and prepared, to the Good King's Home Castle. Before her birth, the contract had been written, the signatures bled.... She was the promised one, the bethrothed of the King's First Son. Through the Son and his bride, peace would come to these nations and the enemy would be vanquished forever.

Paracoeur, the King's loyal liege, surveyed the child. He caught his breath in wonderment, for the Gossamer Child was indeed a child of very tender years. She tottered toward him, clothed in white of a weave at once diaphanous and feather-like with a small circlet of gold, perched like a plaything, on her brow. The circlet was so refined that it reflected only the fire of the Coeur d'Luz perched high above in the morning sky. Her skin was pale, like ivory scraped thin, and her limbs...of a vert, were no bigger round than the signet ring on his finger.

An arduous journey awaited them, the thought of which furrowed his brow. She was like a delicate, gold-crested finch and in no ways as hardened for the journey as he was. This would be a task; a challenging one, at that. Foresworn he was to perform it and so he would or hope would die to this world.

The Gossamer Child stared full into his eyes and in a whispered, prayer-like voice she spoke:

"I kept watch. Was it for thee?"

"Yes. It is I, as was promised."

*　　　　*　　　　*

A lively tune piped to the rhythm of gentle rain that tickled his burnished beard and enticed his senses from the land of sleep. His silver- grey eyes opened to see her perched abranch in a cedar, swinging her legs to the melody she sang. When a lark joined her song with its clear, sweet notes, she clapped in delight with such zeal that she nearly fell backwards. Her wide eyes, ever changing like the brush strokes of the heavens, danced with delight and she clapped again to learn that he had awakened.

"Kind sir, thou hast not taken thine leave. What joy to find thee still ameadow."

"And may the Dawn greet thee, child; I perceive that thy beater is full of melody." He sat up and stretched his arms; refreshed, unhampered by neither the noct's length nor his bed of meadow herb.

Her cheerful eyes did not hide from his greeting as she scampered down the cedar to dance a step about his feet: "I am wondering of thee. Thou art not like all the others I have seen...Why? Why have I waited? Why hast thou come? Where hast thou come from? Where dost the Dawn sleep?"

"Thou art full of queries! I be here enton with thee, as I was bid. Where I come from thou wilst not soon see. I come and go as I and the King will it. Thou hast journey of thy own to consider, Little Maid."

At that, Paracoeur, the King's Liege stood and stretched, yet again. His were limbs lithe with perfectly tensioned muscles. He shook the rain drops from his shoulder-length hair. His countenance was smooth-skinned and held a bronzed hue of youth that belied the many Coeur d'Luz passes his silvered hair gave hint to.

He had taken rest clad only in azure doublet and breeches, for the meadow of Nunatok was secure. It was a sanctioned refuge and had been held so, at King's decree, since the battle had ranged to these lands. He hastened enton, because the rain grew bolder, to don his fine-twined linen cloak. White and of robe-length, it was edged with exquisitely card-woven broideries of blue, purple and scarlet; the cunning work of inspired weavers. The cloak was a gift from the King and the King's Liege wore it with great affection. That it provided comfort in all weathers and was empowered to take no soil was of added benefit on journeys. Since its gifting, he had included it in his daily wearing. Because of the cloak's length, he girded it with a stiff woven leather girdle wrapped several times round into which he tucked up the ends of the cloak so that his legs could move unimpeded. The girdle was inscribed with uncommon words and attached was a scabbard for his sword; though, he preferred to keep the blade in hand.

This meadow being sanctioned ground, he had removed his shods shortly after entering, though the two stood ready to be stepped into at meadow's edge. Barefoot, he crossed the cool carpet of meadow herb and stooped before the child where she enton sat demurely on a rock. His hands dwarfed her tiny feet as he gently cupped them. How slight and tender-skinned they were!

"This will not do, Little Maid," He cooed softly.

The King's Liege strode back across the meadow to where his poke hung from the ancient cedar that his shield rested against. From within, he pulled forth a soft lambskin fragrant with oil.

"Little Maid, comest forth and stand upon this skin for but a brief." He called as he laid out the lambskin, skin side to the grass.

When he beckoned, she gaily half skipped to his side, and his face was warmed to a smile by her manner. His good humor always lay close to surface and in haste he grew fond of her, the Gossamer. He took a sharp of honed steel and deftly traced around her feet on the soft lambskin.

"Hop off, Little Maid," he smiled to himself again when, but two briefs later, he saw how minikin the lambskin soles were. Why, her feet were scarce one third his palm-length! In his palm, there kindled a single greenflame which he lay gently on a quartz stone.

“Liege" she called, from where she plucked fleurs off their stems, meadow's edge "In what brief shalt we ajourney?

The King’s Liege paused from his work. "We can not depart lest our preparations be rightly ordered, Little Maid."

Then, carefully, he held the moccasin soles just above flame’s leap so that they were wrapped in the smoke that wreathed above the small fire he had coaxed from the greenflame with cedar shavings.

"But, I pant to embark!"

Paracoeur laughed a laugh from deep in..."Of a vert, Minikin Maid, thy gossamer feet have traversed naught but meadow herb. Thou needest a cloak and headgear, as well. We shalt ajourney through no sanctioned meadow.

"Tell me, Liege, how to call thee? Tell me, of what length is the journey? Of what fragrance is the bosk outmeadow? Is the sky as clearly blue and the meadow herb so green? Why must we ajourney and where do we ajourney to?"

"Thou mayest call me Counselor, and that is enough of questions. All will be answered in due time... Ah, these are smoked sturdy indeed, enton...." The cedar smoke had tinted the soles pearl grey and had stiffened the lambskin sturdy, but still pliable. “Engage thou in merriment while I seek solace and guidance in contemplation during this pass of Coeur d’luz. Young Maid, it would never do to ajourney without soul prep. And to leave before the acquiesce of Time is to invite adversity. Each day’s wort is sufficient without our added foolishness, dost thou not agree? There is need also to attend to mine weapon and shield. When the noct comes, I will sew thee some mocs, like thine feet have never dreamt of."

Later, at noctide, the Gossamer Child nestled in his own King's cloak, her breathing rhythmic and feather soft. The King's Liege had built the fire up with a cedar branch dragged in from northwoods of the meadow.....he had built it, more for the comfort of beater, than the warmth of flesh. His silvered head was bent over tiny moccasins, as he adeptly laced the moccasin sides with sturdy strips. The firelight flickered upon the Gossamer's head of flaxen, wispy curls and filled the meadow with the sweet incense of cedar and the clean, sharp scent of lanolin from the leather scraplets that he had fed into the flames.

* * *

"Art we rightly ordered, enton?" Gossamer paused in her song, hushing the harmony of the bird song that had filled the cedar-shadowed meadow only briefs before. The carpet of meadow herb sparkled with the dawn's dew and the Gossamer child idly plowed her toes through its plush growth as she stood, arms held behind her back, her face coyly tilted upwards toward the face of the King's Liege.

Paracoeur finished fastening on his Golden Breastplate, and answered quietly "Not quite, Minikin."

Gossamer's gaze fell and she watched as her toes began to rake the meadow herb roughly from right to left. She peered up; storm swirled in her darkened blue eyes which were almost buried beneath her furrowed brow.

"Hmmpf." Her delicate hands fluttered to cover her cough and she peered up at the King's Liege again.

Upon the edge of his great, double- edged sword, Paracoeur's eyes were trained from between narrowed lids. His silver-grey eyes intently traveled the sword's span. He seemed to be unaware of her presence.

"HmmmPF!" Again, a cough, a bit louder than before, her hands clasped tight in front of her gape.

She walked heavily to the meadow's edge and peered into the thicket beyond; straining her neck as far as she could into the cleft between the cedars.

Paracoeur sheathed the great sword, stroked his beard and eyed her.

Her feet danced-quick, little, stabbing steps over the threshold of the forest's edge. Although she did not ken it , he watched her even still. His gray eyes noted the petulant, un-piped tune she danced to.

A pout played around Gossamer's lips and her darkened eyes darted once again to the King's Liege.

When her eyes caught his gaze, a plaintive sigh spilled from her beater to the patient counselor. "Before thine arrival, dear Counselor, I had happy here. I forgot that I wait'd for thee.... I never long'd to ken more than I have...but, enton........" her eyes edged with tears. "I can only ken how empty I will be if I stay."

"Indeed, is it so, Minikin?" He stroked his beard anew.

"Yes...and my dreams are frightful: filled with dust and grime and nothingness. My beater pulses so hard that it awakens me."

"Aye, this I ken" For indeed he had held her, wrapped in his cloak, a palm-full of nocts, and had hovered over her fitful moans from the land of sleep.

"Oooooh," The child crumbled face down to the grass.... She sobbed and wailed, her tears joining the dew of the grass. "I ken not how to tarry, my beater longeth to commence"

Paracoeur cooed "There, there, Minikin, little lambkin...it doeth no good wise to wort thyself afeard...." He knelt to scoop her up in his arms but the child suddenly jumped up and clutched him.

"O, please, Kind Sir, Kind Counselor, Paracoeur, do not depart and forsake me here" she pleaded.

He warmed her in his strong embrace until the waves of her sobbing ebbed and she rested, quietly exhausted with her face against his chest. Softly, oh so softly he cooed to her in comfort: "Nay, nay Little Lambkin....I will not leave thee or forsake thee...nay, nay I have bound myself to thee with the scarlet cords of oath, for His sake....and for mine own."

When, at last, she lifted her head to gaze full into his face with grateful solace, he flipped back the broidered edge of his cloak that draped over his shoulder hiding the murex- colored poke that hung there. "Now, dry thy face upon my linen cloak and give a smile, Child, for I have a gift for thee."

Her face brightened.

The King's Liege prized out a small, white bundle from his poke; a fine gold cord was intricately wrapped about the bundle like a net.

She fairly pranced before him "What is it?"

He presented it to the child with a flourished bow.

"From thee, O Counselor?" delight streamed from her eyes.

"Nay, I have brought it, but it is sent by the King's Son by order of the King."

She turned the netted bundle end over end, peering at it closely and then shrugged her tiny shoulders and handed the bundle back to him.

With one finger, he deftly touched a hidden clasp on the netted cord and shook forth the folds of a beautiful milk-white, fine-twined linen cloak.

"Oh", she clapped in glee.

"It is a King's cloak. Put it on, Minikin. Enton, let me help."

Obediently, she clasped her hands over her breast and turned so that he could drape the cloak about her shoulders. "A King's cloak?" she pressed the soft linen to her cheek.

He fastened the gold cord net under her chin. "Aye, only those pledged to the King are gifted with such," the edge of a smile hid behind his beard, "and no one enters his presence without one."

The Gossamer buried her nose in the cloak's crisp, clean scent "Be I pledged to the King?"

"Minikin, ___thou hast been promised through bled signature and the King's Son desireth to have thee as His own, but only thou canst pledge thyself. Methinks thy tears bespeak thy beater in this matter. Does lex of thy gape accord with that beater of thine?"

Gossamer's ivory face grew solemn and her eyes widened: "Is He as kind as I want Him to be?"

"Aye, kinder"

"And… good?"

"Aye, he be the very good of good- fearsomely good."

"Is He the King I envision, the King I desire Him to be?"

"Time will only tell; but this I ken: He is the King of thy greatest need."

"If mine lex and mine beater pledge in one accord and I be clothed with the King's cloak, might I see Him?"

"Thou wilst not only see Him, thou wilst live in His realm for all cycles of branch.

"Aye, I do."

Paracoeur aptly drew the cloak over her crowned curls "Thou dost what?"

"I do pledge mine self to the King and His Son….." Gossamer peered into the Counselor's eyes: "and to thee."

"Enton, let us lace thy lamb's mocs." He knelt before her as she offered first one foot and then the other. He laced the pearl grey lambskin tightly up almost to her knees. Gossamer danced a ginger step or two in her new mocs and laughed out loud.

Paracoeur stood upright and tightened his sword's scabbard. The meadow was full in the alt pass of Coeur d'Luz. The Gossamer waited in laced lamb mocs and milk-white cloak while he latched his bronze shods upon his feet and took up his giant shield from its resting place beside the aged cedar. Clasping her tiny hand in his right hand, he led her to the thicket's edge.

"Enton, art we rightly ordered, Counselor?"

"Aye, to the King and mayest thy path be straight, Little Lambkin."

With those words, the Gossamer and the King's Liege stepped together into the thicket. The meadow behind quickly faded into shadow and the path before them opened upward; though the span of it was hidden ahead by the darkened woods.

The leather braided cords stretched taut from the yoked oxen to the ancient, but well-sharpened plow. A man, muffled in rags, was hunched over the plow handles; struggling, pushing and grunting as the oxen strained to pull the plow through the hardened soil.

Rain drops ran down his face, joining his sweat and forming little rivulets through his beard. Soaked to the skin, he pressed forward, throwing his weight against the plow. This field had lain unused for time upon time, hard-baked by the glaring suns of many Greenbranch. But now, this field held the promise of harvest. It was all that remained. The rain beat harder, bouncing off the stone-hard soil and running inch deep along the field until it fell over the far edge into the roadside ditch.

The man reared back, forced a deep breath into his crying lungs, and flexed his body for an all- out assault against the plow handles. The oxen balked frequently and needed to be encouraged. Oblivious to his ebbing strength and rain-soaked misery, he was obsessed with urgency.

The latter rains had begun and the field was not yet prepared to receive the seed. There was none other in the village able to strain alongside him. His forehead was bloodied and the blisters had long ago burst and rubbed raw through the skin of his work-calloused hands. Yet, he single-mindedly pressed forward; urging the oxen to pull. The field must surrender to the plow, must yield up the soft, rich loam beneath the rock-hard surface.

Nothing else mattered. Mud and manure splashed in his face.

He was the stranger. His roots were not here.

TWO

purple cord

Dusk flitted moth-softly alongside the trail which stretched white against the fading pass of Coeur d' Luz. The Gossamer's tiny head rested in the crook of his arm. He trekked upward. There was little reason to linger. Although they had been a whole Coeur d'Luz pass on trail, they had not traveled the distance the pass should have held. Of certain, her legs fair trembled after the many lilting skips she had made to keep abreast with one of his strides. The first pass of Coeur d' Luz had held great marvel for the small fragile bundle that was enton tucked under his cloak. The tip of her nost was saffron-dusted with the pollen of fleurs that she had paused to smell along the way. Like a new, nost-led whelp, she had wandered round about him; off the trail here, over to a wondrous sight there....

A smile had sported beneath his beard edges often. Surely, he was strong in the virtue of patience, it was of no wonder that the King had set him upon this quest. His timeworn power of patient endurance would not be tested by this effervescent child. He hurried enton, released to his own pace, kindled by his foresworn pledge. The rhythm of cricks echoed his lengthened strides, masking the deep rumbling which whispered throughout the surrounding bosk.

Velvet black shadows began to wrap his steps as he trudged onward and upward. All during the pass of Coeur d'Luz, he and the child had pressed toward the peak of Nunatok, or he had pressed as firm as the tender one could be pressed. No sooner had the Gossamer glimpsed the candle breath aside in the thinning trees and dashed ahead in exuberant frolic, then, of a sudden, she had crumpled verily into a little pile of exhaustion and fallen fast asleep mid trail. Not being sanctioned ground, the King's Liege could not strike camp there and he had gently scooped her up into his free arm and increased his pace. Noct was indeed upon them and even though the forest was sparse here nearer the peak, Paracoeur was deeply aware of the lurk within the shadows. Not wishing to go to battle with child in arm, he fairly flew along, scarcely grazing the feldspar gravel of the trail with his shods. It was not possible to move about soundlessly in bronze shods. Never had it been his way to hide his goings; should Danger seek him, it would find his sword well- honed.... Clearly enton however, his shods betrayed their whereabouts and fair signaled to the denizens who dwelt always on the edges. Alas, never had it been his way to travel nor fight with a child in arm … ah, for the fervency of youth, or even a swift steed.

He could sense the shadows, creeping always closer. Snarling, the denizens snapped at his heels. Let them get a mouthful; of bronze, that is! Eons it had been since Fear had dared to stalk him. Had its memory grown dim? Such a trouncing he had given it. No arm in the Kingdom matched his sword arc. Were it not for this child, Paracoeur would walk the darkened trail as if at noontide, without challenge. Enton, like cats to the mouse, they pounced at heels? Had he the pride of youth, he would have taken offense at their slight. But Paracoeur knew it was not he that these darklings sought.

Moving even swifter, he shrugged the huge Golden Shield riding on his back, higher onto his left side, protecting even further the wee one who slept still in his arms. Thanks be to He, the child was soundly exhausted and not awakened in fear. Flexing his hand about the hilt of his sword, Paracoeur held counsel with himself. Neither at this time, nor at this place would he choose to vanquish. The Gossamer Child's safety was of greater import than giving foes the sound thrashing their foolish arrogance deserved. Although his right arm fair trembled to be cut loose from reason's restraint, he turned off trail instead. Through the branches he could see the candle breathing heavily from the Eremite's window, a lance throw from their foot trail. Even enton, the wizened sage beckoned from yawning door.

The King's Liege burst into the small hut causing the hearth fire to quiver and the candle breath perched on the windowsill to breathe its last. He gently laid the sleeping bundle on a small pile of clean straw near the hearth. Turning, while taking his great Golden Shield from his back, he gripped his sword and rushed back out of the hut. His leave taking was so abruptly strong that the door was slammed by the wake of air that followed him.

The Gossamer opened her sky-glass eyes and sat up blinking. Sleep had frosted its crust over her lashes and she had to rub them with her tiny fists until her gaze was free to wander about the room she found herself within. Weathered-grey log splits chinked with a deeply amber substance mirrored the fire from every angle around the room, making it seem the whole ablaze. She clutched her limbs closely to her body and prepared to shriek in fright. Out of the corner of her eyes, she caught view of a wizened ancient sitting on a stool. He sat quite at ease with his aged hands resting calmly on his white robed knees. He was gazing at her, but when his eyes mirrored the fire, they twinkled as if they, themselves, contained candle breath. Curiosity climbed up from her little rumbler and she lost her fright as quickly as it had jumped on her back.

"Greetings, Good Sir," she had noticed his robe of the King's weave and instinctively knew she need not be afeared.

"Bid welcome, such a wisp thou art to hath captured His heart," the wizened one spoke while stroking his silky, white beard with a deep chuckle.

Her eyes opened wider still. His voice was like a mix of honey and oil, poured slowly into her ears; it cloyed sweetly in her beater long after the sound of it had fled the room. She stared at the ancient one with sky-eyes wide and she edged a bit closer.

"I ken thee not, Sir. Perhaps thy eyes see another, " as her voice warmed, the lilt of her chat increased in speed enticed to gaiety by the sweet warmth stirring in her beater "It is like the dawn in here. The fire plays tricks on thine eyes.

He laughed outright from deep within his rumbler. "Nay, Child, I have the keen eyes of the peregrine. It is thee whose eyes are blinded from the light. "

The Gossamer's eyes widened and sparked for a brief and then she scrambled to her feet trying to gain her balance on top the tumble of straw. She crossed her arms in front of her chest. "Sir, I do so see that thou art quite old with mine own eyes."

He laughed deeply again. "Clothed in fledgling pride and the King's robe? I see with mine keen eyes that thou art much more of a dilemma than a wee gossamer. Calm thyself, Child; we will not talk of things too large for thee. Thou hast slept well, on trail?

Disarmed, she sat plop down upon the straw again.

"Of a vert....I don't ken, for first I was there and enton I be here. And He, mine guide, is not. He made mine mocs, dost thou likest them? How came thee by a King's robe?" She scrambled down the great pile of straw and ran to his knee. "Hast thou been to see the King?"

"Fair Child, the King is the oldest of friends to me. Come here to the hearth and warm thy limbs by the earthen tiles. It pleases me to brew a tea for thee of warmth and vigor. I ken of thy journey and it would be wise to be warmed and full of vigor.

The earthen tiles radiated such heat and the room so blazed with the fire's reflection, that Gossamer was surprised to find only a little, merry, cedar fire set upon the hearth. She sat obediently on the stooped hearth and watched. The Eremite walked sprightly about the room opening several drawers of a cedar chest and drawing forth a palmful of pungent leaves, a small clay pitcher of milk and a pot dripping with honey. Pausing to throw the long strands of his beard over his shoulder, he minced the leaves finely with a small, silver sharp and wrapped the shards of herb in fine gauze. He poured the milk into a granite kettle and twirled a honey dipper seven times round above the kettle. Amid his wrinkled face, his lively silver eyes studied the liquid amber as it slowly spiraled from the dipper into the kettle. Then he added the gauze of herb shards to float upon the milk.

When her hind side began to feel over-warmed, the Gossamer turned to face the fire. The little, merry fire in the hearth surprised her once again with its flames for they were alive with color much like the bow in the sky after the rain.

"Venerable Sir," she ventured, "ken thee where the strong Counselor art? We paced upwards toward the peak, but enton I ...he..., I shut my eyes for a brief and he hast vanished. This is......quite a niggle for me...first he is there and then ...he is not."

"Hast he not foresworn thee? Why niggle? Didst thou not grant him boon of trust? Methinks thee, Gossamer, have much to learn about the King and His Liege. He is closer than thee ken, of a vert." Placing the kettle on the hearthstone to brew, the Eremite continued. "Come, the shadow lurk hast been cut to deep slumber, let us stroll out to view the heavens."

"But, where is he and when will he come for me? I fear I be left to mine self. How shall I suffer such a journey by mine own stead?"

"My word, what a sprite thou art! Foresworn means foresworn. Thinkest thou that the beater vanished from thy chest just because thou cannot see it? Thou art alive,

Child, after a midnoc trail and thinkest thyself abandoned? He is closer than thou imaginest and about the King's business, as well thee shouldst be. Imagine, a whole kingdom awaits the arrival of such a one as thee and thou hast not the ken to grant boon of trust to he who is foresworn. I shake my head to think how this will bode upon thy journey." Turning back to the cedar cupboard, he drew forth a silver mug, placed it on the hearth beside the kettle and sat down upon his stool. There was no smile in his eyes.

Great shame stole up from her grey mocs to her golden circlet; but she kenned not why- the old man spoke in such riddles she had not the slightest glimmer of what he had said. She kenned his eyes rebuked her, however, and she felt crushed beneath their somber stare. The Gossamer hung her head and her pale face shadowed. A tiny crystalline tear traced the curve of her cheek. Her lips pressed together to form a thin line. The hearth was warm enough, but the walls had become like brass. She was discomfited.

For his part, the Eremite closed his eyes and became like a carved stone. Briefs crawled slowly by and she began to think of bursting beyond the door. The merry little fire seemed too hot, enton. A run on the trail was surely more welcome than this. She shouldered out of her king's robe and let it carelessly slip to the floor. It was altogether too warm inside this hut.

Of a sudden, the Eremite's eyes flew open and he rose quickly from his stool. "Come; let us stroll to the peak, Young Gossamer."

Had he read her thoughts? Gossamer shuddered as she made haste to shoulder her king's robe. Already, the Eremite stood before an opened door. She scurried behind him, but he turned and placed his arm upon her shoulder, pulling her forward until she stood at his side. The silver mug was in his aged hand.

"Drink and be quenched to refreshing. There is little warmth beyond this door. Thy journey to travail is far. And the Dawn has not yet shaken the noct off of her skirts."

She drank obediently from the silver mug, although its rim held heat from the hearth and fairly burnt her tender lips. She dare not cry out; the Eremite, she had decided, was not to be trifled with. A stifled gasp escaped, nonetheless. The brew was at once warmly sweet and boldly bitter. Her sky- eyes widened. The brew's warmth blazed a trail down her gullet. When the brew hit her rumbler it sent ripples of nausea which washed ever widening to her very edges. The Gossamer grasped her mid and her eyes narrowed, dulled like a gale tossed cloud. She folded, like a tunic, towards the tile.

The Ancient One stood half in the chill from beyond the door and watched. His eyes were, at once, deeply dark and shining. He lightly grasped her shoulder and she found her legs and grasped his robe like a lifeline.

"Venerable Sir, methinks thy brew is too stout. Kenest thou that I be a bare, wee gossamer, perhaps I shalt be ill?" Her voice trembled quietly as she held tightly to his robe.

"Let us set forth together and reason while we pace," He nudged her forward and together they stepped outside through the door. "Ken thou much of thy journey?"

"Nay, Venerable Sir," The waves of nausea receded and she stood more upright with every step until her fingertips barely brushed his robe. "I ken it is far...and periled...."

Before Dawn began its blushed, timid stroll across the sky, the Ancient Eremite and the fragile Gossamer ascended to a rocky outcropping near the very peak of Nunatok. Far beneath them, a quilted valley spread distantly beyond the foot of Nunatok. Multi-shaped patches of muted grays and bosk-greens were edged with barely discernable dark stitching. Gossamer clapped her hands sprightly, for here and there, great patches of twinkling stars lay in the valley. Never had she seen the like. The stars clung to the ground like dew to meadow herb and she was delighted with the sight of them. With solemn stare, the Eremite followed the Gossamer's gay eyes to the source of their delight.

"Nay, Gossamer, hath I not told thee as we walked that the valley doth not hold what it appears to. Why clap thee at the sight?"

"Ancient One look! There are stars captured in the folds of yon valley! I be greatly comforted," she continued to chat gaily, "In the meadow, my home on this very mount, those stars have sung to me from afar through every noct since reckoning. Lullabies; ever so softly, those very stars soothed my soul and swept my lids to slumber. I enton have no fear for I ken that my own bosomed friends live within the valley. I thought them distantly kind, but enton I see I shall ajourney to them. Thou trembleth me, Ancient Sage, with thy talk of lurkings. Didst thou not ken? The stars visited me each noct since I was ...."

"Child!" The Ancient One trembled with gravity. "I have spoken that the valley doth not hold what thou imaginest. I spoke with vert. Do not discard so lightly that which is too large for thee." He grasped her slight chin with his aged hand. "Look at mine eyes, Dear Wisp, there is no guile within them. Thou must walk far around the twinklings that lie within the valley. Thy friends, they art not. It is naught, mirrored in deception."

In vert, the Gossamer' eyes strained to focus on the old man's face. Faintly, she remembered like a whisper that he was not to be trifled with. She watched his face with shaded eyes, keenly aware of the twinklings that flirted beyond the edges of her vision. Inside her mid, her beater wildly danced...her friends were near, within her path. Verily, she did try to gaze into his wizened, wisdom-drenched eyes. Alas, her beater enticed her eyes to steal a peek at the twinkling valley stars.

When she forced her unruly eyes back upon his face, there was nothing to gaze upon but the morning mist. The Eremite had vanished like dew in the toasting warmth of Dawn. Gossamer glanced here and there to see his back, but to no avail. He had gone and a slight shudder stole over her limbs, but she shook it off like a robe from her shoulders. Looking again to the valley, the twinklings began to blink out, as well; leaving the ever brightening quilt that blanketed the valley's expanse. She sighed and stumbled to a rounded rock to sit and think and sigh.

"Ho, Minikin Maid of Nunatok!" Paracoeur rounded the trail's bend and leaped the outcropping, just as the Coeur d'Luz bronzed above the far peaks. He fairly shone in her presence and the Gossamer ran and fell upon him with many hugs and kisses.

At village edge, he bent to wash his hands in the run off from the ditch. The rain fell heavily. Opened-eyed, he lifted his face to the darkened sky; the shower washed over his grey eyes and down his work- stained face like the tears of a sorrowful child. His clothing was torn. His body was bone- weary and filled with searing muscle strain. His shoulders bore the telltale stoop of tenacious toil; he looked aged beyond his years.

Alone, he had ploughed the field and later led the oxen to shelter. Before he crossed the ancient road to the crumbling village, he had stabled and foddered the oxen. Even though he was weary, he took the time to clean and hone the plough edge.

The lane was deserted; huge muddy puddles filled the space between the small stone huts. Here and there, rubbish had floated by until it collected in tight corners. A smoke-laden mist hung low and writhed around the huts within the village. The smoke rose reluctantly from smoldering, wood-spent fires; dull red embers nearly buried in ash. The stranger knew this village well enough that he did not stumble as he walked though the pass of Coeur d'Luz was near complete.

He stooped low to enter a crumbling hovel at one edge of the village and was weakly welcomed by a bone-thin man slumped against the rubble.

"My bread is thine, faithful friend." The man lifted a trembling, graying hand and continued, saying:

"Misfortune hath left me little to share, but what art mine is thine." The old man's shallow breaths filled the hovel with a faint gasping sound: "Thou art soaked, Dear Friend, and smell of earth and sweat. Where hast thou been on this baleful day?"

"Simeon, I hope this noctide finds thee well." The Stranger's greeting had a deep and soothing tenor. "I have been afield, this pass. The soil longs for seed. It has been barren too long."

"Thou tookst an ox to field, today? It was not a fit day for man or beast," Ancient Simeon eyes widened with surprise.

The Stranger sat down in the hut and rubbed his huge, scarred hands over the worn knees of his ragged trousers. "It was a damp day," he admitted, "but the field cries for seed."

"Well, The King knows the village needs a harvest. My grain barrel is nearly empty. If I wert younger, I would labor beside thee. How my eyes long to see the field white with harvest."

"No doubt, thou wouldst, Simeon. No doubt, thou wouldst. Have faith, dear friend, a while longer and the barrel will overflow. Simeon, I come seeking seed. Hast thou any to devote?"

"Ah…I'm afeared I have eaten nearly all my seed grain. There was little I could do, besides." The emaciated man spread his withered hands with empty palms upward. "The rats must eat, as well."

"It has, indeed, been long since Greenbranch." The Stranger nodded, understandingly.

"And Barebranch rushed," Simeon continued, "and hid the bud deep within its crusted snow. I might have a few kernels, there, in a small poke behind the kindling thee kindly brought before. I don't know how good the seed be, moths may have supped."

"Brother Simeon, the kindling shouldst feed a fire to warm the chill from thine bones." The Stranger admonished and began to lay a fire on the hearth.

The old man nodded slowly and watched him with dull, spark-less eyes. "I am very weary. Time has drained the elixir of youth from me." Simeon's weary voice faded to silence.

The Stranger bent to blow upon a spark, coaxing the flame to life. Carefully he nurtured the fire, while the old man dozed. The Stranger took a dented copper pot from a shelf and held it out the hovel entry. In no time, the steady rain filled it full. Soon, the pot sat on the hearth, next to the fire, brewing a tea from some rosemary that he had pulled from his own poke. He quickly tidied up the hovel and then laid his own fire-dried cloak over Simeon.

When all was tidy, the Stranger picked up Simeon's scant, moth- nibbled poke and peered inside it. He poured the contents of it into his hand. A cloud of dust puffed up in his face, making his nost screw back a sneeze. When the dust cloud had settled, five whole kernels of wheat rested in his palm.

"I'm sorry, Dear Friend; it is all that I have to share." A weary voice cracked thin through the hovel and the Stranger turned to see Simeon's humble eyes resting on him.

"There is no shame, Simeon. Thou gavest thine all. That is a boon worthy of a king. Here," He lifted the copper pot to Simeon's pale lips, "drink in. This brew will strengthen thee and fill thee with the visions of thy youth."

The old man replied "Rest well this noctide, for thou hast been kind to an old, worthless man."

The Stranger put his index finger to his own lip: "Hush now, Simeon, and rest. Of a vert, thou art honorable and worthy of the king's notice. Fare well, this noct, Noble-Soul. I go abegging seed. For me, rest will come when the field is sown.

Simeon nodded and waved a half wave before his withered hand fell limply in the lap of the lent cloak and Simeon dozed once more.

Outside again, the rain had slowed to a drizzle. Drippings from every eave filled the noct air with a staccato beat sounding much like the lively percussion of night frogs. A restless specter, the stale smoke, crept upon the Stranger's nost and clung to his damp hair, as he went from hut to hut abegging seed.

Some huts, with roofs fallen heavy upon broken walls, held no light at all, with nary a voice to call back a greeting to his knock. From other huts, built of mud brick that had worn down like long- abandoned ant hills, the frail replies from plague victims hastened his step.

In one such, a widow named Anna offered him a weak tea, the color of ditch water. He drank it, gratefully, while she searched under her mattress for a hidden poke of barley seed.

Near the village centre, where the huts were larger and of hewn stone, he was turned from a few doors like a despised tramp.

"Perhaps there is work, the next village over."

"Peddle thy wares, elsewhere… friend. Thee will'll find no manna here."

Occasionally, a frightened voice whispered through the door boards, "Flee, Stranger, lest thou be overtaken with the plague."

When he was invited, he entered humbly, bringing wood or herbs to the weakened hut dwellers. Once, he brought a fire breath cupped in his huge, scarred fists to spark a hearth that had long ago grown cold.

"How didst the day spend with thee, Mary? Is there any seed to spare for the harvest next?" He called from a respectful distance outside the hovel of the village harlot.

A woman burst through the entry and fell weeping in the muddy puddle at his feet. She was wrapped in a scarlet cloak which quickly grew heavy as mud and rain seeped into its weave. The Stranger gently touched her arms and lifted her to her feet; but, her eyes remained downcast.

"Kind Stranger, thy question hath graced me exceedingly. I don't have seed; I have never had need to plant. But, take this…" She stretched out a hand laden with a heavy gold chain. Her eyes full of wonder as she gazed upon the face of the man who offered respect and asked only seed in return.

The Stranger shook his head and with his giant, scarred hand cupped her fingers back over the chain she offered: "Thank thee for thy kindness, Mary, but I can not plant gold.

"Please, Kind Stranger, I have no use for this. It is a weight around my neck. Tis a vert, I am not strong like I once was."

"Nay, Mary. I have no need of gifts or gold. I need only seed to plant the field." He looked steadily into her brown eyes, which pooled with tears.

"But, Kind Stranger," Mary pleaded, melting in his gaze she fell to his feet once more, "I want to help and this is all I have."

Again the Stranger bent and gently lifted the woman. "Thou hast more than thy account, Mary. If thou desireth to spend thy strength, as well; walk over the tor and use the promise of the chain's worth to rent a coach. Thou art no stranger to the coach stop. Ride to the next village that clings to the King. A smithy will break the chain for thee. Dismiss and pay the coach…with gold only and…."

"But Master, I can not leave. There is quarantine. I wish not to carry this plague to yet another village."

"Mary, thy fever has been broken, thy wounds have dried. The plague canst not hold all its victims. Believe me when I say, the only thing thou wilt bear away from this village is good will. The world need not be afeared of thee. Purchase barley, some dried fish and, yes, some honey and perhaps some ewe's milk for the children. Find a bale of rosemary. Hire a cart from that city and send it laden back to the field. I will…"

"Yes, as thou hast said , that shalt I do. I wilt hasten to return with thy goods."

"Nay, Mary, thou must not return to this village. Purchase the provision I ask for and send it back.'

"This is my home. I will not be welcome to stay elsewhere." Mary bent her gaze to the muddy puddle beneath the mucked bandages on her feet

The stranger cupped her chin with his huge, scarred hand and lifted her gaze to meet his. "Make this thy home no longer. Take courage and believe what I speak. Enton," the Kind Stranger reached into his poke, pulled out a small, flawless white stone and held it out to her. "Take this to the King's storehouse in that village, present it at the gate. Thou wilst be welcome. There are looms there. The Weaver, he is no stranger to me, will teach the honorable trade to thee. Thou must learn to work well with thine hands. Some here will need cloaks to endure the approaching Barebranch. "

Mary's eyes clouded with puzzlement for a brief and then, trembling, she reached for the offered stone and quickly placed it safe within her bosom.

"Go," he smiled broadly. "And, Mary… with the chain that remains, after thou hast sent what is asked for, purchase a white linen gown of thine own.

The trembling woman brushed the mahogany curls from her face and glanced down at her gown, drenched and spattered with mud. She blushed deeply and turned to go but he reached out and placed his hand gently on her shoulder.

"When I send word, come to where I am."

As Mary hurried away splashing as she ran toward the ridge beyond the field, He turned to knock on one last door.

red cord

The faint cadence of her beater echoed in her ears. She could not remember the count; or how long since she had last been aware of its beat. She lay still, staring silently up at the dark nothingness. Or ...were her eyes sealed shut and she in her grave only remembering how the agony before death had strangled her last breath. She could not discern her state. Once, memories had swirled above her, just beyond her mind's reach. When? How? But enton, she had not strength enough to lift her palm and feel for the lids of her eyes. It did not matter. Eyes closed, eyes opened. Miserly darkness engulfed her; perhaps this would be the last echo her ears heard.

Nay, what sound coaxed her ears to hope again: a slight rasp, the grate of stone against cold stone? She strained to hear… not even needing to hold her breath. Her lungs were scarcely active. The slow cadence of her beater grew loud within her ears as she tried to harvest sound from the deep, starless dungeon she lay within. Iced, iron chains weighted her weary body to the stone cold floor. Slowly her mind formed a thought: it was only the chains' scrape that she had heard.

Raging fire, a wild-eyed steed, galloped un-reined through her broken bones. Pain burned within, like a fire unquenched leaps from hearth to chinked wall and greedily devours a home; without mercy or regard to boundaries. How odd to burn while lying on the arctic stone of the dungeon floor. There it was again: a rasp;

the grate of stone, perhaps? Mustering strength from the deep- within the chambers of her beater, she tried to will her body to obey and turned her eyes in the direction of the faint sound.

A crack of light pierced her vision like a rapier, thin and deft. There, beyond the top of the age-worn flight of stairs that she could see clearly outlined, daylight boldly penetrated the darkness of the dungeon that entombed her broken being. Bright light charged through as the chipped, black obsidian door opened wider. Step by worn step, the light bolted down into the dungeon routing the darkness that retreated into the corners and imperfections of the roughly hewn rock chamber. Then, the darkness folded in upon itself and formed a wall from the landing downward. Like a bulwark, the darkness braced itself against the light's advance. The light slowed like a reined-in battle-steed to a march, a steady advancing cadence determined to ram itself upon a gate.

Reminiscent of a dying butterfly fluttering to lift its worn body from the ground, her eyelids blinked rapidly but she moved not. Astonishment sobered her pain-sopped brain. Where deep, darkest nothingness had been, dust particles enton twirled and danced wildly in the light of a beam from Coeur d'Luz . Quite still, she lay and watched the dervish dance above her. She struggled not against the heavy, iron chain that pinned her down. It was enough to watch in wonder as the myriad hues of rock and light became uncloaked above her. Her beater jumped a beat as if to join the dust dancing in the light of Coeur d' Luz and her thin lips trembled into a slight curve, a barely perceptible smile. A solitary thought surfaced though her wonderment: perhaps the light would stretch its march to warm her limbs.

She ken'd not how long the dungeon had held her chained in its bowels. There was no way to count. Starless darkness remains ignorant of passing time and finds no measure in the cadence of a dying beater. Enton, one thought sparked another; for hope is mystically powerful in that way: "if only".

"If only," she thought, "the light will reach to touch away the deep chill that slows my blood...If only, I could feel its warmth...."If only," she strained to see the light which had slowed its advance down the steps, lingering long on the worn step, second from the bottom.

"If only," her thin lips silently gaped. "If only," she dared to whisper. The thought of the light's warmth encouraged her and she carefully tried to lift her bone-thin finger.

"If only," she spoke, her voice thin as a hollow reed, "I could reach it." She inched her finger toward the bottom step, still weighted down and tightly grasped by the iron whose cold links bit her flesh as she tried to follow her finger with an arm. "If only," she paused and studied the angle of the advancing light. "If I can summon even an ounce of will to move towards the step, I ken I will feel thine warm embrace, Light."

THREE

blue cord

He knocked upon the thick, timbered door of the village council chamber.

A voice intoned through the grey and peeling door. "Who knocks at so late an hour, on such a night?"

"I am come to gather seed for the planting of the village field."

"Hast the plague stolen thy mind? The field is as stone, cold and barren."

Another voice escaped. "Go, take thy fevered rest; we will see to the needs of the village.

"This very day I have taken the oxen to it. The furrows are straight; the soil begs for seed."

What?" The thick wooden door flew open, creaking harshly. "What pretence troubles thee? Why…thou art but a stranger?"

Hands stabbed out from the shadows within and drew him roughly inside to the council chamber. The sweetly stale air within the chamber suddenly shrouded him, like the windowless room of a dying invalid. He had to choke back a gag. He tried to look into the eyes of those who had pulled him within; but, the room was filled with shadows and urgent, angry whispering.

"Who gave thee permission to plough in the village field?" a faceless voice demanded.

"I came and knocked. No one answered. There is no grain. The children starve… I lent my back." His broad face smiled, reassuringly: "Do not worry. I demand no boon, no wages. Any good man would've done the same."

He was aware that someone else's hot, rank breath was filling the air which he breathed. There was a great deal of scuffling and scraping until someone managed to light the lamp which hung from the ceiling. He was not entirely surprised to find his view blocked by a pocked face that framed an impeccably, trimmed beard neatly edging ochre-stained teeth. Eyes, murky and scruple-less, scrutinized him closely.

"This is grave, indeed!" The gape spit more, hot, rank breath at him. "Thou hast no authority to do so. The village tenets are specific concerning trespassing."

The stranger respectfully lowered his head in the presence of an obvious official. In doing so, he saw that the Official leaned heavily upon a polished cane. The Official's feet were bound up with yellowed cloth strips through which bloodied pus seeped incessantly.... The plague haunted the council chambers, as well.

Taking a step back, the Stranger surveyed the room, aided by the sputtering oil lamp. The men who crowded around him were dressed in once-fine togas but there was nary a one who stood firmly on his own two feet. Some leaned upon canes, most leaned heavily upon one another. All were weak and bandaged, but each had a neatly manicured beard and a head waxed with pomade.

"Enton," A wave of compassion swept over his face and the stranger fell to his knees and took herb from his poke. "Let me tend thy wounds, this herb will draw out the poison that rages within." He gently took hold of the Official's sodden, bandaged feet.

"How dare thee! Get thy common hands off of me!" The Official sputtered in astonished rage and shook the Stranger's grasp from his foot.

"Who dost thou think thou art to plough our field and touch our wounds?" Another jerked the Stranger to his feet, nearly losing his own precarious balance in the process.

"Kenest ye from whence I come?"

His answer shocked the room silent. Slowly a great murmur began to swirl up the chamber walls.

"Impertinent, ken thou not where thine feet standeth, enton?

"It is not fitting for the stranger to plough the village fields."

"It is unlawful to tend the sick without a permit."

"His very actions accuse us of malfeasance and we are but sick and dying."

His steel stare sharply plunged through the yellowed eyes of the Official. His lex stilled the stormy, tumult. "What larder stores thine tithe? In which house doth the tax dwell? Is it lawful to chide a stranger when stands no advocate?

"Silence!" The pock-faced Official roared. "Thou hast not been recognized in this council. Thou hast not been granted boon for lex before the council. Thou dost not have the right."

"He has no regard for procedures." One proclaimed.

The murmuring began to swell again and rise in volume.

"…Is his name on the birth rolls? He canst not speak if his name be not listed."

"How brazen, first he tends to our poor and now he attempts to touch the Official. Is there no end to his disregard for proper convention?"

"He is a law breaker!"

A calm voice floated up amid the clamorous tumult: "Nico, thou keenest the lex is just. No stranger may stand in counsel without an intercessor. It is forbidden by the King's decree.

The pock-faced man turned and spat: "The King? Thou wouldst quote decrees to me? Thou art my old friend, but art unseemly impudent."

The clamour banged anew. "He has no business here in this village!"

"By whose authority didst thou enter the village field?"

"And he hath collected seed that wast not his own."

"… he meaneth to steal it away to the next village."

"A thief! A thief disguised as a stranger!

"Under whose authority?" the voice demanded a second time.

The Stranger stood straight, his gaze faltered not. "Thou wouldst ken."

"Do NOT instruct me. I am the official of this village. I ken what is to be ken'd!"

The Stranger cleared his throat and stated clearly: "Evidently the scroll of decrees has been misplaced, since thou kenest not the King's decree of hospitality."

"What thinkest thou of thine state? How darest thy brazen lex? Dost thou not see we are all taken by the plague? And yet thou plagueth us with obscure decrees and troubleth our field with thy insolence." The Official's face grew red with rage and suddenly he began to hack a deep and hollow cough that caused him to wobble uncertainly.

The Stranger reached out with both his huge calloused hands and steadied the Official as the cough gave way to spasms.

The crowded council grew hot with anger and the press of infirm men massed around the stranger amid shrill cries.

"Cast him out, he dost not listen to reason."

"He toucheth our Official and quoteth little known decrees. Throw him out!

"Nay," A lone voice sliced through the clamour for but a moment. "Mercy, he is a stranger, he dost not ken our plight," but the reasoned voice was soon dulled in the din.

Of a sudden, the room was filled with hacking men who held each other tighter and leaned against the walls to keep from collapsing. The clamour died, swept from the chamber as some surrendered to heaving, breath-struggle. Others leaned forward to dab at their oozing, bandaged feet. The Stranger had vanished from the chamber, but few noticed his absence and fewer still remembered his entrance.

The thick, wooden door slammed swiftly .A village elder had struggled against its weight while taking his leave from the council chamber. Once outside, the lone elder leaned heavily upon his cane and looked fervently up and down the crooked rows of huts and hovels. At the edge of the last row, he spied the Stranger. Pulling a hood down over his face and bending over the polished wood of his cane, the elder struggled to pull his misshapen feet through the muddy puddles

"Thou followest . Why?" The Stranger stepped from behind Simeon's crumbling hovel into the path of the elder.

"I am familiar with the decree of hospitality." The lone elder leaned wobbly upon his mud-spattered cane. "And there is no law against kindness."

"Thou art in need of some kindness?" The stranger probed.

"The village is in need of food," the elder turned his eyes down to the muck which soaked through his bandaged feet "… and we are weak….thy back is strong."

"And what wish hast thou?" The Stranger paused. "How canst I help thee?"

"I am weary beyond measure." The village elder sighed. "Help me to my hut and sit awhile. Thy voice is clear, thy mind is free from fever, I perceive. I wish only to sit in the company of a right mind....

"And?"

"And I have seed which cries for a field. It will never find its way there upon my feeble back."

Hours later, when the moon hung high in a rain-scrubbed sky, the Stranger sloshed slowly across the road to the field. The moonlight cast a silver glow around his silhouette. Tears rained down his cheeks from his heart that was deeply clouded with sorrow. It seemed the weight of the whole village was upon his back. Of a vert, the poke upon his back bore only eight measures of seed. In his hand, he carried a mud spattered cane, a gift from the elder whose fired hearth he had shared that evening. It would make a good planting stick.

The links of iron had more substance than the wisp of flesh and bone that she had become. Still, she ken'd: "If only" was all that she could grab at and so she pushed against the chain's weight to leverage a thrust; a move toward the light. With everything left, she gasped and stretched in a great, heroic effort which stirred a dust cloud from the stone cold floor. Alas, it was too short to bridge the gap from where she lay to the bottom stair that had slowly, inch by inch, become bathed completely in the bright light, right before her light-starved eyes.

There was no more strength within her and she smiled a weak smile as the hope which she had struggled to hold onto became a mocking irony. She would die soon. This she ken'd. Her beater raced, fed by nothing, to carry her to nowhere but a grave. She would perish on the cold, dust-covered, stone floor less than half a stride from the warmth of the pure light of Coeur d' Luz.

Her beater slowed…one…two…her breath ceased for several briefs. She willed her eyes open and held the lit stair within an unblinking stare. She tasted another shallow sip of air, dank and moldy, on her parched lips. Far away, as if beyond a heavy veil, she heard the clamor of the marketplace. Another muffled beat of her weary, muted beater; another sip, so tiny, of air dripped into her lungs only to be swallowed by the collapsing vacuum that crushed within her chest. One wee sigh fled with the slight, oxygen- starved breath from her lips; but her gaze remained fixed on the light which appeared to beckon.

Of a sudden, a long shadow stretched down across the steps. Fear dared to clutch its icy fingers even tighter around her throat. She could not fight, she could not flee. Her eyes sought the door above the stairs. A figure, largely bold, blocked the light from Coeur d' Luz that streamed through the doorway. A breeze blew down the stone stairs and filled her lungs afresh. And she saw sparks erupt as obsidian shards were crushed beneath bronze shods.

From her perch on the peak, she marveled as the stars below her lost their enticing luminescence and blinked themselves, one by one, from her view. Like the slow imperceptible blossom of a fragrant flower, the pale light of Dawn began to gently sweep the noct from the corners of the lowlands that stretched before her. Surrounded by a gray stillness, she glanced at Paracoeur, who sat beside her on the rock outcropping. Her beater quickened its beat and burned a little. Paracoeur was silent. He burnished his great sword in the half light. The song of Dawn rose with bird-song crescendo, surrounding them both in its symphony. But Gossamer did not smile; she pined for the meadow, which had been her abode stretching back before her reminiscence. Gently the Dawn greeted them as it peeked over the gray clouds. Even the Gossamer's customary child -like chatter was hushed to stillness by the sky that blushed before them.

"Kind Sir," she whispered, "the light begins to burden my eyes, dost thou ken that we should hide behind these rocks?"

Paracoeur paused in his task and looked directly into the light which had begun to emerge, stark and naked, casting aside a cloak of clouds. A gentle smile brushed across his lips and he bent to his task again without a word.

Squinting in the harsh glare with her hands on her hips, Gossamer ventured again: "Dear Counselor, the light brightly smarts mine eyes, perhaps we shouldst move into the shadow behind us?"

Paracoeur paused once again and glanced at the maid beside him, with a puzzled look: "Little Lamb, how be it that thou wouldst shun the Dawn? One should never court shadows when the Dawn dances her splendor before thee." He lifted high the freshly burnished sword, strong light flashing from it in all directions, and inspected the sword's blade, with eyes wide and undisturbed by the light's strength; peering closely to see if any mar defaced the sword's surface.

She cried out, her eyes fast filling with tears, as the sword flashed before her and she raised the corner of her King's cloak over her head. "Paracoeur, I want to leave this perch, the light burneth and maketh mine eyes to cry."

He turned to face the small fragile child who shrieked beside him. "Why? Do not shrink from that which is cleansing, Young Maid. Look fully and permit the Dawn to enlighten thee. If the eye is full of darkness, the whole being shall be engulfed in it."

Gossamer scrambled to her feet, ducking all the while and hiding her eyes behind the cloak's edge.

"Thou soundest like the Ancient Eremite; Thou speakest in riddles while mine eyes run water and are pained." She stamped her moc'd foot and fled from the outcropping to stoop behind the boulders. "I would rather this rock falleth upon me than sit by thee and look while Dawn breaks mine eyes with her lightsword.

Protect me, as the King foreswore thee!" She demanded.

Paracoeur stretched his lithe limbs and stood, half-tempted to laugh. He sheathed his great golden sword and stretched out his hand toward the crouching maid. "Come forth," he invited, "The Dawn dances her awe for thee, be not afeared. The pain is good and will clear thy sight."

"Mine sight needs no clearing, save from the rudeness of her naked glare."

"Come forth, at once." He chided. "The lady is no foe of thine; thou mistaketh the intent of her brilliance."

"Lady?" she asked, pursing her lips, she glared at him from eyes narrowed to mere slits, "Nay, methinks a harlot. She shouldst clothe herself!"

"Come out, thou art acting like a haughty child. Such lex dost not befit the gape of one promised to the King's Son. Where findest thou such a lex-hoard, in sacred meadow, no less?" His outstretched hand warmed to point in her direction; but, he restrained it, on account of her youth and his blood oath.

She clambered out from behind the rock and glowered straight at his bearded face. "Haughty child? Like a haughty child?" She questioned. "Hmmpf! Her bone-thin arms were crossed like a tight girdle across her heaving chest. "Thou makest mine beater thick with gall. Is that meet for a protector?

"Peace, Little Maid, thou art troubled in thought and beater. Breathe deeply and steel thy gaze to embrace the light of Dawn. I am foresworn, it is not I who bringeth harm to thee." Paracoeur turned his eyes fully toward the young maiden and his eyes searched hers deeply. "Methinks thine beater is asmolder and is bitter, clogged with ash. Tell me what troubleth thee." Her beater lay plain and unclothed before his gaze, but the King's liege knew that Gossamer had not perused her own beater. It is common ken that the young do not plumb the depths of their own souls without abet.

A lump of indignation rose up her throat and she lowly growled: "Hmmpf. Thinkest thou that I am troubled? I am fine, just fine…" She turned, scrambled back over the rock and sat with her back turned toward the Liege Knight and the Dawn.

He waited.

A huff of air escaped her throat and she tightened her arms across her chest.

He waited, his face calm, his eyes reflecting the Dawn.

"Thou carest not for me!" a whispered whine rose above the rock.

Yet, he waited.

"Mine eyes burneth whilst thou playeth with thine sword. And thou art called my guide?" Her hands were fisted, held tight, close to her chest. "Who dost thou think thou art? Think thou art the only guide who treadeth mine meadow? Thinkest that the many passes of Coeur d' Luz whilst I waited for thee, I spent alone? I had many who would give me counsel and play." She stood and turned to face him. Her words ataunt: "Thine friend is a whore who parades around the sky with no shame, no covering, and she hurteth my eyes. Doth the King kennest that thou keepest court with such harlots at my expense?"

"Thou exceedeth thine boundary in ignorance! Thou scamper about the rocks, having left thy proper modesty behind, and darest to speak of the King's servant, as such?" He thundered. "Get thee here at once and drop that filth from thine gape. I've half a mind to thrash the seat of thine ignorance with my girdle!" He had not lost his good humor, yet he marveled at how this small being could so foolishly try a warrior's patience.

"Well," she indolently continued, "Thou discardeth me with that strange old man; abandoned by my own guide. I have kenned that harlots keep a man from his duties."

"Gossamer, it is not meet to hideth from the contents of thine own heart by attacking else where."

The Liege Knight was actually calm of spirit and enton hid a smile beneath a sigh. He spoke to the air "Oh King, I lean upon thine strength, this child doth not comport like a royal. Her gape is filled with basurlex and her eyes prefer the darkness!" He looked far across the valley to where the stark whiteness on the far mount sparked with brilliance; a signal fire which bespoke to him of the King's forbearing character. He sat down, shaking his head. "Thou kennest well." He spoke again to the air acknowledging that the King was wise to have set him upon this task.

But, the maid was not so moved by the sparkle of white from far across the valley. She stood, stiff necked with thin arms across her chest; the white, woven cloak fluttering behind her to the ground.

"I awoke and thou wert gone." She accused, a bit louder. "The Ancient Eremite shivers me; his words art strange and I ken them not. Thou makest mine beater smolder" she stated icily. "Twice, I have been abandoned in mine need by thee."

"Twice? I? Thou hast lost thine reason, perhaps because thine eyes are dark- loving, thou canst not see clearly." He looked again, full upon her.

She shrank not. "Yes, in the very first night of journey, thou threweth me; abandoned without a word, upon a pile of straw …"

"I didst not leave thee alone."

"…in a stranger's hut..."

"The Honored Eremite is not a stranger. He is the King's own bosom friend."

"He was strange to me." She kicked at the pebble in front of her moc, bruising her toe." I was frightened; thou wert nowhere to be seen." Narrowing her eyes she accused him: "Thou abandoneth me. I am just a wee gossamer, so soon gone from mine own meadow. Thou art so big;" she accused. "I am quite little when thou art not by my side. How couldst thou leave me, whilst thou sported in the noct?"

Paracoeur held his steel grey eyes in place, lest they roll, and placed his giant hand upon the shield that rested against the boulder that he sat on. His good humor forbade the heat to court his beater and pity filled his next words. "Little Princess, I was not at sport in the noct forest. It is not for thee to demand account of my time and deeds. I am the Liege of the One, True King. He trusteth me as thy protector. If thou canst not see everything, thine eyes being darkened, canst thou perhaps not remember mine many kindnesses toward thee? Would the cobbler of thy mocs, the strong arms which carried thee whilst thou didst sleep, so swiftly abandon thou to frolic in the night? Methinks thou shouldst attempt to apologize to the Dawn, who only sought to balm thy eyes- sorely cluttered with sleepmat."

The Gossamer lowered her flushed face and surveyed her mocs intently. "But, thou didst not give care when the light stung mine eyes. Thou didst nothing. Thou couldst have raised thine shield."

"The point escapeth from thee, Dear Miss; the light threatened no danger to thee. Shouldst I, thine foresworn protector, protect thee from that which would be to thine benefit?"

"It hurteth mine eyes. I do not like it."

"Thou dost not ken it. The pain is necessary for the cleansing."

"The light in far meadow never stung mine eyes."

"And thou saw no farther than the edge of the bosk surrounding it. One who would ajourney must take sight of the path and the destination. This is of a vert that can not be disputed. Oft times, pain walks alongside great strides. So long in thine meadow, didst thou not ken? The King requireth courage in his subjects." An amazing gentleness flowed from his eyes and warmly washed the chill away from her dulled sky-eyes.

The wee Gossamer lifted her head from her bruised toe and surveyed the bearded face of her counselor. It was as if she melted in his gentle gaze and different warmth wrapped her beater. "Well...."

Paracoeur took her in his strong arms and sat her on his knee. She tried to squirm a little from his grasp but could not stifle a giggle when his silvered beard tickled her. His silver-grey eyes mirrored the light of the Dawn, like a serene mountain lake, and reflected that light into Gossamer's. He brushed the sleepmat from her eyes, careful not to damage her fragility with his huge war scarred hands. She shuddered and surrendered the whole of her small body to lean hard against his chest. Turning her eyes toward the glow of full Coeur d'Luz that enton filled the sky, they sat together and watched as the glory of Dawn fully crowned, exposing the canyons which seamed the verdant and brown patches of the quilted valley below them.

When it seemed to Gossamer that the whole pass of Coeur D'Luz had rushed by them, she suddenly jumped from Paracoeur's lap and began to scramble among the rocks.

"Let's go! Let's run down to the path!" She shouted gaily.

"Wait, O Little Fount of Impatience, methinks thou hast forgotten something." Standing, he bent to retrieve her white woven cloak, brushing the reddened dust from its broideries. "Do not rush to the broad, bent path. We must follow the brook down. Firstly, let us slake our thirst full from yonder cool spring."

"I can't drink. I am not athirst. The Eremite gave me brew to drink in the noctide." She scampered back to Paracoeur's side. She grabbed the pointer of his right hand and sought to pull him toward the path with her. "We can drink later, we should hasten to the path; our journey grows old while we sit!"

"Nay, Young maid, thy impetuous nature will surely dry our journey. Drink full, till the ag laps up against thiner beater. This spring which sits upon Nunatok's brow is clear and clean and wilt brace thou well for yon journey. Coeur d'Luz will soon parch the bounce right out of thee.

Paracoeur instead pulled her along by his pointer until they stepped on the mountain herb circling the spring. He knelt and cupped his colossal hands, plunged them through the sun's reflection on the spring's surface and brought them again to his bearded gape, drinking deeply. She watched, amazed, that he could gulp such a measure of ag at one time. When he cupped his hands again beneath the spring's surface and held them to her slight gape, she smiled and shook her head and the gold circlet from her head tumbled into the spring. She pounced at spring's edge and lapped the water like a lep; almost choking, the ag being so crystal cold.

Gossamer plunged her tiny hand through the spring toward the circlet that glittered from below and tumbled in after it. She splashed and sputtered ag until Paracoeur's beard was fully sopped and he grabbed her by her frock lifting her with little effort from the frothed spring. Totally ag whelmed, the Gossamer continued to sputter and choke as Paracoeur carried her dangling by her frock to a flat, ray- warmed rock and plopped her down to dry. He sat down and laughed until his belly danced beneath his doublet and he, too, gasped for air.

"Methinks, I said to drink, not swim." He held his aching sides.

"Methinks it is not mirthful. I only meant to retrieve mine circlet, not dive into the spring." She wiped the rivulets streaming from her darkened ringlets down her nost and tossed her head, which sprayed his beard again.

"Methinks the spring is deep beyond thy grasp and thou hast surely slaked whatever thirst should parch at thee this pass of Coeur d'Luz. Come, thine cloak will soak the flood from thine frock and the sun will warm thee. Thy limbs are purple enough to be threaded through the broideries on thiner cloak's edge." He wrapped her cloak about her and hoisted her to his broad shoulder. In three strides, he crossed the rock outcropping, grasped his broad shield and slung it over his other shoulder. His face was split with a broad grin when he plunged off the cliff's edge to follow the brook as it raced from the spring. Gossamer shrieked with half delight and grabbed tightly at his silver- stranded beard, lest she tumble from his shoulders. She had been startled by the great distance from his feet to his shoulders and held tightly to the beard as if to rein him from a trot.

It was many briefs before they reached the straggling bosk of stunted cedars which climbed toward the rocky point of the peak. The Gossamer began to nod and sway from her perch on the Paracoeur's shoulders. He reached up and removed her, tucking her under his right arm as he quickened his stride and leaped from boulder to boulder alongside the brook. The air smelled of wet rocks and the spray from the brook's playful jig kissed at their faces.

From her view parallel to his jumping feet, she dangled limp, seeking to satisfy her curiosity. Her nost swung level with the Great Sword's scabbard and she trained her eyes to study it inch by inch. The scabbard was woven of soft, supple leather; a white and tenderly intricate weaving. Within the weave were set twelve stones of many hues. The stones were cut in the shape of six-sided stars. One stone, a deeply glowing blood stone, drew her attention. It seemed to pulse and lay vivid against the white weave of the exquisite scabbard. The texture of a raised vine climbed through the weave and seemed to continue unbroken onto the girdle which the scabbard hung from. The girdle was fashioned from stiff leather. The twining vine trailed the borders of the girdle heavy with etchings of ripened fruit. Uncommon markings were deeply inscribed into the center of the gold - brushed leather girdle. Gossamer was sure that these markings formed a message of some kind but she had never learned the skill of discerning soundscript.

She glanced up at Paracoeur and shuddered. He was a massive sort and she felt very small as she swung from where she dangled. She surveyed the great gold-brushed girdle again and recalled Paracoeur's words from the peak: *I've half a mind to thrash the seat of thyr ignorance with my girdle!* Her eyes widened. The girdle was immense! A distinct, cold tickle began to creep along her backbone and whisper to her brain: "How very big, much bigger than thee ...dost thou rememberst how his eyes darkened when he didst chide thee on the peak? Perhaps he will surprise thee with a great wrath...Thou canst not tell what he wilt do; as the King's Liege, he surely canst do what he willeth...."

Of a sudden, Paracoeur interrupted his swift stride and swung Gossamer up to gaze into her eyes. He smiled broadly and questioned: "Hast thou dried from thine spill ...and now begun to take a chill?"

Startled more by her own thoughts than by his sudden action, Gossamer smiled shyly back. "It goeth well with me. Perhaps, Kind Sir, I could find the solid ground beneath mine mocs. The height of thine knees giveth me unease."

"Of a vert, the ground here is solid enough for wee mocs. And we have traveled well, there art briefs to spare." Paracoeur gently placed the Gossamer down and continued: "Walk at the edge of the bank, the rocks art not too slippery there and the stones art such as wilt not discomfit thee."

Taking her hand, he slowed his pace and they walked at brook's edge for some briefs. The Coeur d'Luz was climbing on his pass through the sky and the high air was glow-warm. The cedars which marched the mount were of greater girth here and seemed to hug the sky with their tall branches. Here and there an odd conifer with speckled awl filled the air with a piercing, cleansing scent that caused them both to breathe deeply. The herbage also was of a different sort, with tufted fronds that were laced with tiny fleurs. She was delighted and pulled free from Paracoeur's warm grasp to run and press her face fully into the tufts until she began to sneeze and her face emerged dusted with pollen and smiling.

He rumbled a laugh and beckoned her back to brook's edge. They walked together in silence for a space and then she queried; "Why here walk? The brook's edge is hard and oft times sharp."

"It is best to follow the brook that leapt from the heart of Nunatok's spring."

Placing her fragile hand above her face, to shield her view from the glow, she looked deep into his eyes and continued "How kennest thou this? Hast thou ajourneyed here before?"

"I am well journeyed, Miss, and there are conducts befitting the road." He ceased his pace and looked back into her face, the eyebrow lifting above his right eye.

Gossamer turned from his gaze and began to walk languidly beside the stream. "Well, methinks the flowered tufts have a softer path to tread!"

"Methinks they do not journey far as thou dost, Little Miss. Dost thou grow weary? I can bear thee up for a time. I had hoped the lamb mocs would cushion thy footfall."

"The mocs suffice, but yonder in the trees is soft and fragrant and I doth grow weary of the mist clouding my eyes and kissing my cheeks."

"What a blushing, shy maiden, thou hast become." He chuckled and he shifted his shield in order to lift her to his back.

"Nay, I am weary of riding; I want to run through the bosk."

"Ken ye that the path to the throne does not wander through this forest."

"I will run within thine sight. I need to frolic with the fleurs and collect petals for a crown."

"Thou hast a crown, Dear One! Disregard the brook and walk thou with me; I will shield thee from the spray."

"Methinks the trout will nibble off my toes, if I lose my step and splash in their home."

"Thou wort for naught, the trout art a friendly sort. "

They walked on, she pulling free from time to time to fetch a stone or pick a fleur and he waited with outstretched arm for her return. It seemed more like a Kingsday ramble than a commanded journey. Be it of a vert that Paracoeur, himself, might have longed for a plunge into the bosk. The steepness here at brookside did not tax his agility; the stone did not challenge his step. At ease with whatever surroundings he found himself in, he longed always, nonetheless, for the home courts. Of a vert, he longed to carry the small maid both to bring her small feet rest and to quicken their journey. The sooner his own shods entered the King's courts, the more satisfied his heart would be. He had grown to treasure this impetuous child, however, and would indulge her fancies, should they not spell a danger that might ensnare her. Sensing that hunger nibbled her to distraction; he walked from brookside to spread his great cloak on the leafy carpet beneath a spotted awl tree.

She stood brookside and watched him with cocked head, Coeur d'Luz' stood altpass and his bright light shone harshly from directly above them. Had it not been sifted through the bosk's emerald canopy, the ivory-skinned child would have been seared crisp. She reflected that, as far as she could see, it was as if she were viewing the bosk through a thin, translucent leaf. The air was awash in green hue. She breathed deeply, filling her lungs with the vivid air and then ran to plunk down on Paracoeur's spread cloak.

Like magic, he had produced a small flame from a wisp of awls, after using his huge hand to scoop a small fire circle from the leafy carpet. Leaving the single flame to send its faint smoke spiraling up through the canopy, he went and bent near the brook. He tucked the silver strands of his hair behind his ears, his forehead etched with concentration as he made careful study of the brook's ripples. Of a sudden, he plunged his hands beneath the icy ag and brought his hand up, cupped, with five small shiners swimming in it.

"Thank thee for thine sacrifice, my friends". He whispered gratefully.

From his poke, he drew a small, copper bowl, poured the cupped agarium into it, and placed it kin to the well - disciplined flame. Paracoeur polished the great golden shield with a flourish using the sleeve of his doublet and placed it in the center of his outspread cloak. Once more he fished into his poke and drew out a gauze-wrapped package. Carefully, he loosed the gauze wrap and stood three, tender, aromatic loaves, warm as if fresh from the ola, upon the golden serving platter.

Meanwhile, Gossamer scrambled to her mocs and began to flit from one tufted frond to another; selecting beautiful fleurs to strew on their altpass table.

The fragrance of the bosk was faintly smoke and wonderfully green, as they banqueted on the feast of the three barleyed loaves and five shiners. When they had both professed to eating their fill, Gossamer was surprised to find two handfuls of crumbs left

"How is it, thine rumbler is filled with so little?" Gossamer queried. Scooping the crumbs into her wee hand, she was about to scamper about to toss the crumbs for the birds.

Paracoeur, however, stayed her with his right arm and then pulled a scroll from the breast pocket of his doublet: " I have food which thou kennest not." He, while rolling out the scroll, pulled her onto his lap.

"Come and sup with me this tasty sweet; like honey it is sweet to taste, like milk it will grow one strong."

She stretched her neck to peer at the strange markings which lined the scroll. " I can not hear the soundscript with mine eyes, strange markings they art to me. How is it that their whisper is not silent to thee?"

"Ah, Little Maid," he peered into her eyes," methinks thou hast sleepmat still. Had thou made yield to the Dawn, the marks would speak quite lively to thee enton. Come; let me attend to thine eyes in this matter." He leaned forward, rubbed both his eyes with the backs of his giant hands and then blew a gentle breath upon them. Then, he made an even closer study of Gossamer, filling her whole view with his own eye. Gently he salved her eyes with his palms; rubbing them with a light massage while he aimed a puff of his sweet breath onto her face.

She startled back and blinked. Eyes open wide she looked again upon the scroll and began to read. "Look, Paracoeur, the markings are speaking to me as if we had spent many a pass together!" She exclaimed.

"Ah, if thou wouldst listen carefully to the sound symbols, thou wouldst hear the aged tale of how thou camest to be upon Nunatok in the sacred meadow.

"Yeah, and I see it has much to say about the King and his hidden garden."

"Take much heed, Promised One, and thou wilst have a pleasant journey. Keep the scroll, I have another." He gently lifted her from his lap and stood, towering over her like the spotted awl bosk that surrounded them. "Wouldst thou be content to feast upon the sweetness of the scroll and stay seated on the cloak? I must survey the trail which beckons to us." He took his great shield, returned to brook side and turned to speak once again. "Stay until I return for thee. The cloak is spread, should too much supp put thee to drowse. Do not wander, I will return before the noct begins to spread its shadow."

Gossamer nodded in reply, too apt in the scroll to give Paracoeur her full attention. She unrolled the scroll and devoured more and more until her soul was satisfied and her eyes grew heavy. She made a nest within the great cloak that lay spread upon the leafy carpet and curled up, pulling a corner of the cloak over her. Snuggling into drowse, she surrendered to the warmth of the day.

The birds were singing a new song when she awoke. With a smile she leapt up and remembered the remains of their lunch. She began to toss a handful of crumbs up into the branches above her. Out of the corner of her eye, she saw a slight movement. Turning, she saw only a fleeting shadow. She stopped feeding the birds and watched the woods around her intently. Returning to her task she tossed another handful of crumbs up to the songsters. Again, she thought she saw movement skirt her view. She paused again and was about to re-roll the scroll and sit down to wait when she saw, surely, a shadow dart behind the spotted awl tree. Gossamer stood on tiptoe and stretched as far as she was able to see around the broad trunk of the tree. Almost falling, she took a step to the right and stretched again. Before she was aware of it , she was off of the outstretched cloak and clear on the opposite side of the tree trunk.

"Oh my!" She said when she noticed how far from the cloak she was. She decided that she must leap back onto the cloak without a moment's delay. Mid-leap, she again thought she saw a shadow flee to the right of her. Twirling quickly, while still in the air she caught sight of the shadow just as it disappeared behind a tree about six strides away. Her feet in a tangle from misdirection, she tumbled to the soft leafy carpet and fell nost first into a clump of moss. It smelled of age and earth, but in an instant she was up and running. "Just a peek," she thought "perhaps it is a bird at play with me. "

On she larked from tree to tree; round this tree, round that one, she tried to tag the bird, which was always a shadow stride before her. Gossamer giggled and plunged round a spruce hoping to trap the elusive shadow. She wanted to trap it and thank it face to face for such a delightful romp.

"Come out, come out, wherever thou art!" she teased gaily and began to skip with great abandon, round and round the trees.

On the far brook side, Paracoeur stood, shield and sword in hand. His face was grim, his eyes sad. He watched in silence as the frail girl ran to and fro; farther and farther from the outspread cloak. He watched as she poked her head within the knothole of an ancient cedar and whistled a bird song. Ever ready he stood, while the girl skipped farther from her appointed place. Shaking his head, slowly, he crossed brook side and knelt to empty the copper pot. He packed it and the gauze loaf-wrap back into his poke. Grabbing the corners of his magnificent king's cloak, now crumpled into a forgotten pile on the forest floor, he shook it free of dust and crumbs until it blew like a banner in the growing breeze. Throwing it over his shoulder he strode toward the sound of the Gossamer's laughter; away from the brook and into the darkened bosk.

Her chest was in playful breath-struggle when she collapsed at the foot of a tall poplar tree. Laughing and flinging the leaves which covered its roots, nearly a whole handspan wide, she giggled and buried her face in the bark of the tree.

"I will hide, now, and thou canst find me, shadow bird." Throwing her cloak over her head she began to count;" one, two, three....six...eight...ten...." Her voice echoed back to her, sounding empty and hollow.

Carefully she peeked from under her cloak and half expected the shadow bird to leap and tickle her. But the bosk was silent. She glanced around and did not see one fleeting playful shadow. The poplar was surrounded by many trees and their shadows covered the ground. Gone was the dappled pattern from the pass of Coeur d'Luz, which had tattooed the forest floor with warmth and joy. The air held a deep chill. She clutched her cloak round tightly and thought to return to the cloak at brookside. She looked this way and that, but saw no cloak, no brook. Her head cocked as she listened for the playful brook song. The bosk remained ominously silent. Even the bird song had ceased. As she listened with a panic climbing from her rumbler to her throat, only the distinct, rapid beating of her own beater could be heard.

Like a dawn that shyly disrobed her clouds, ken crept in slowly. She was lost. All at once, the trees seemed dark and like a solid wall built around her. She looked up and could only see a darkened green that roofed this grove with no window to the sky. An angry, olive-colored moss grew thickly everywhere and filled the air with a dank, moldy odor. Gossamer sank down until her frock covered her ankles and drew the cloak even tighter.

"Rooawhhh! Rooooawwhhhh" a throaty howl erupted behind the poplar tree. It curdled her blood afeared and made her beater drum. The resourceful maid sprang from her crouch and grabbed hold of the poplar. Up she scampered like a squirrel frightened by an owl.

"Rooawhh! Roooawhhhh" Gossamer peered from her perch in the tree to the ground below, looking for the horrid beast, which had frightened her so. About thirteen strides from the tree, she heard the rustling of brush. Perhaps it had gone. Perhaps it lay in hiding, waiting for her to descend. She squeezed the trunk tightly and noticed that the wind had increased. As the tree swayed, so didst she. Perhaps she would fall.

FOUR

red cord

A rush of wind threw the pressure of weight from her lungs. Clearly the bold and brawny figure began to descend the dungeon stairs. A great clank of blade upon blade startled her, causing her to gulp deeply of the metallic-tinged wind. Above on the stairs -a battle raged; blades against shield. Clanging metal echoes bounced from the dungeon's rock walls. A great struggle ensued that sent wave after wave of fresh wind into the cavernous chamber; with each breath, her beater increased its rhythm. The clash of steel upon steel crashed upon her ears. As the melee descended the stairs, her vision grew clearer and panic began to pound wildly at the door of her beater. Dark guards battled a lone, brave figure who wielded a golden, two-edged sword.

Above her, sharp steel bit and parried against heavy iron shields. She strained to discern the features of the golden-shielded warrior, who battled the horde of dark guards pouring through the gaping door. Alas, his back was toward her as he stepped backward, one by one, down the worn, stone stairs. His sword swiftly flew to meet the stinging weapons of the swarming adversaries.

He stood as still as the trunk of the tree he leaned against, his azure doublet and breeches clearly in view, as his fine twined cloak was thrown over his left shoulder. In one battle-scarred hand he held a huge golden shield, in the other a striking, double -edged sword. Around him the bushes responded to a gentle wind, but only a strand of his silver hair danced slightly against his bronzed features. The expression he wore was slightly bemused. The tree he stood guard under was a lithe, virgin poplar with a trunk grown wide from many rings of growth. The noct had come and gone as he had stood guard. High above clinging to the swaying tree was his precious charge.

She was shrilling his name and had been for most of the night. He had been answering her through the night and even moments before. Doubtless, she heard him not; perhaps because the sound of her own voice filled her ears, or maybe her white twined cloak was wrapped too tightly around her head.

There was no danger; although he stood ready, as was his nature. Perhaps soon her voice would grow hoarse, or her rumbler would speak of its hunger and she would come down and discover that he had been always here.

"Paracoeur!" She shrilled again. "How be it thou standest there without giving answer to my beckons?

He glanced upward and barely saw her sky- eyes amongst the leaves. "How be it thou hast lost thine ears, Minikin?

"I am hiding here from the grave danger that lurks below." She continued to shout: "Take care, Dear Counselor lest thou become sup for such a creature."

"Come down. The danger thou hast perceived journeys far from here enton. I await to escort thee on thy journey."

Gossamer began to rustle in the branches above and proceeded to climb down the poplar. Midway, she lost her grip and began to slide as an otter on a mud bank. The woods were alert to her screams. Paracoeur remained unruffled and expertly caught her in his massive arms, before she broke her fall upon the ground.

"Dost thou prefer the tops of trees to the King's spread cloak?" He queried, while setting her upright upon the ground.

"Nay, Kind Counselor, I lost myself in a game and had to climb up to protect mine self. The bosk was alive with horrid growls and scurrying shadows! I was almost eaten!" She straightened the gold circlet upon her fair curls and shrugged the folds of her white, tapestry-trimmed cloak from her shoulders. "Why wert thou so late in returning?"

"For a fact, I returned at the appointed time, but thou hadst forsaken the appointed place. Thou must learn, Maid, to obey the rules of the trail."

"I do not ken the rules of the trail. I have yet to put mine moc'd foot upon the trail for thou wouldst traverse down the soggy brookside, over many rocks."

"Where is thine helm?"

Feeling abruptly at the crown of her head, she gasped. "I ken not. The helm was there before."

"Thou must wear it always, I have told thee. Yet, thou speakest of no ken about the rules of the trail? Methinks thou art mistaken. What commands the King of those who wouldst walk the trail?"

The Gossamer paused and placed her finger alongside her nost; furrowing her brow. "....Courage."

"And?"

"To wear cloak and moc and helm....always."

"And?"

"And? --I do not remember!" Throwing herself petulantly to the ground, she began to wail. "Woe is me, Paracoeur...how wilt I ajourney, if I canst not learn the rules of the trail?" She buried her face in a pile of silver-backed leaves at the base of the poplar.

"And ...thou must obey instruction; lest, thou tumbleth into danger. Come enton, we must retrieve our journey before the noct thieves yet another pass from our allotment." Paracoeur stood tall and beckoned her.

"But my helm, my precious helm..." She began to wail anew

"Come now, take comfort. Ken thou that thine protector is sloth to retrieve thy litter? He pulled her helm from his poke and held it out, gleaming.

"Oh, Wise Counselor, thou art ever good to me. Help me fasten it, mine circlet tangles in my hair, if it is not worn properly."

"Surely, Gossamer, the Faithful King's Liege is delighted to attend to thyr wardrobe." He chuckled as he flourished a low bow before aiding her in dressing her hair. "Come, thou hast wandered far from the brook. We wilt have to take yonder trail to catch the brook many strides below."

The day was warm and pleasant, the air full of insects humming. As they walked further down the narrow, rarely used path, the bosk that lined the trail began to alter. Soon there were many broadly leafed trees with only a few awled trees interspersed. These leaves were mostly brightly green, but here and there yellow, brown and even red. The Gossamer was content to hold the hand of her knightly escort for many strides until she spied another on the trail ahead.

Through the side of her mouth, she whispered to Paracoeur. "Behold another on the trail ahead. Shouldst we hide or fight?"

"Neither, we walk ahead like the courtly beings we are until we are abreast with yonder being."

"Ah, and then thou wilst draw thy great sword in sure surprise and vanquish the foe?" She whispered eagerly.

"A frail maiden like thine self is an unlikely challenger, Young Maid. Fightest thou with all strangers? Peace, be still…..the woman is no stranger to me. Act with courtesy and she may yet do the same." He instructed. "Hasten, now I will present thee to her acquaintance." Paracoeur increased the length of his stride, still holding Gossamer's hand, until she fairly ran beside him.

Less than a stride from the figure ahead on the path, the King's Liege ceased his quickening and called to the cloaked being:

"Mistress Rachel, how doth the path go with thee?"

The figure ahead of them turned slowly round to face them, letting the many-colored cloak fall from where it had covered her face. Dark auburn tresses framed a breathtakingly beautiful face with haunting brown eyes. When the stranger had turned, a waft of thick incense had dizzied Gossamer with its heaviness.

Gossamer gasped; surprised to see a woman alone on the trail, but Paracoeur bought her silence with a quick glance.

"Ah, Liege, I thought I heard the wind calling my name." The woman bowed low to the ground, and Gossamer saw a crown of jeweled thorns upon the woman's waist length hair. "The journey has become interminably tedious." She surveyed the child next to him and added bitter sweetly: "On journey afresh, I see. How goeth the path with thee?

"The path is straight under my arrow shods, Mistress. If thou desirest, we wilt gladly share our provision and strength with thee." The King's Liege bowed low, pulling the child to bend as he did.

"Methinks not. I have not the strength to pay the toll the King would surely charge for such a boon."

"Thou art an unwise judge, Rachel, the King would gladly pay boon to thee himself, wert thou only to bow before his throne."

"I have walked his path many a pass with Coeur d'Luz, Liege, and followed all his rules, yet he shows himself not to me and I await still his coming."

"Indeed, thou followest the rules, but thine eyes are drawn ever downward to the path, perchance thou wilt miss him, when he dost arrive."

"This path is king-cursed. Liege," the gauntly beautiful woman hissed "I watch for roots which would stun my feet and trip me hence to tribulation.

From deep in bow, the Counselor replied with a controlled voice. "The path, indeed is blood cursed; but, not by the Good King. Perhaps thou shouldst not be so swift to slay those who greet thee in his name."

The Gossamer began to tremble like an autumn leaf and drew herself fully into Paracoeur's shadow. This woman was more than Gossamer had first perceived. As Gossamer peered out from her shelter, the stranger's face changed, growing more ancient with every brief, until a weary, wrinkled crone stooped before them and began to rasp an overture toward the child.

"Ah, pretty, do not be afeard. I do not eat slight chiblings, only misguided fools who would stray me from my appointed rounds. Come hither. Dost thou like stories?" The Crone pulled her multicolored, patched hood over her graying hair and beckoned to the frail Gossamer with a bony, outstretched finger. "I have stories, the like such as thou hast never heard. Come I will entertain thee whilst we walk."

Gossamer clutched tightly to the sword arm of the King's Liege, but he patiently pried her loose and gently pushed her toward the abruptly aging crone who bent toward the earth like a humped, worn hillock covered with a spread of jewel- toned, brocade patches, once elegant but enton threadbare. Had the thick incense not still hung burdensome in the air, Gossamer would have thought the beautiful woman had vanished completely and been replaced by this ancient wrinkle of a woman. Turning, the frail child buried her eyes in the Liege's King's cloak.

"Nay, child, remember thy courtesy. It is well to hear the stories of she who wanders forever searching for he who is easily found. She dare not harm thee, she kens well my sword." He gave Gossamer a gentle push in the small of her back.

Gossamer reluctantly tread forward until she was abreast with the woman. The cloud of incense weighed heavily on her nost and caused her eyes to tear. The ancient crone grabbed Gossamer's hand and Gossamer began to shrink back. Of a sudden, however, the crone turned her eyes directly into Gossamer's sight and the young girl stood stunned from flight like a deer rapt by a flame nest.

The little maid was surprised to find the crone's eyes richly warm and intoxicating. As the strange woman began to draw Gossamer down the trail, the frail girl became entranced and followed meek and obedient.

Mistress Rachel began to speak "Come, Precious and I will spin a tale of mine journeys and how I came to walk these endless paths…"

At first the woman's voice cracked and rasped but slowly it became stronger and vibrant. Gossamer grew bold to glance again into the woman's face and was surprised to find the olive skin soft, smoothly supple and the hair auburn anew. The cloud of incense faded to become a light, fragrant aura just hinting of cinnamon and myrrh.

"Once," the beautiful woman began, "I was the courted of the King. Although I was slender, my back was strong and I could run these trails with fleetness. He sent me beautiful silken gowns and bid me come to his diamond white palace. At night he sent great columns of fire to torch my way. Daily a cloud playfully beckoned me. He sent messengers to tell me of my beauty. Like a gazelle I was, then, in his eyes."

Gossamer could hear the faithful trudge of Paracoeur as he followed close behind them. She felt safe holding the hand of Mistress Rachel and watching as the woman's face became animated and glowed in sudden splendor. Gossamer's beater began to warmly glow towards the mysterious woman and she had ken of the Great King's courting ways with the radiant Rachel.

Rachel continued: "The King, he is comely beyond compare; full of grace and might, a righteous judge among the people. He walks erect and never stoops to cruelty." The woman brushed the deep red locks from her face and spoke on, a curious whine beginning to frame her words. "He sent me a beautiful letter full of justice and bade me understand that he would come to rescue me in triumph."

Paracoeur leaned forward and solidly questioned the woman. "And what was the justice the King penned to thee, Fair and Favored of Women?"

"Ahhh, I scarce recall, I tore the letter up and left it trampled in the trail." The whine increased.

The small child gasped and shyly removed her ivory hand from the woman's clutch. "Why? Why wouldst thou do so, when thou loved him so?"

Distracted, the woman grabbed the hand of Gossamer without a thought and continued. "He showered me with gifts, fragrances and the fatness of the land. His love for me was strong. I was happy, oh so happy...." The woman's voice fell to a bare trace and then they walked in silence for a stride. Gossamer was ever aware of the steady tread of Paracoeur following behind them.

After a space of time, Paracoeur queried in his strong, clear voice. "Bethinks, fair Rachel that thou played the harlot then?"

She turned and spat back at the King's liege, grasping Gossamer's flesh tightly. "I was beautiful; couldst I help the many swains who came to ply me with attention? Art thou so lifted up that thou wouldst deny me the taste of wine from other goblets? Perhaps the paramours were greater than thy King? Certainly, they were timelier."

Again, Gossamer gasped and sought to draw her hand free, but the woman held tightly, deeply pressing her painted nails into the girl's ivory flesh.

"Careful, Little One," the woman warned roughly. "There is a rock there which would send thee sprawling." Jerking Gossamer's arm abruptly, the woman stepped off the trail. "Come, there is an avenue here which is smooth and much traveled. Thy mocs will not last long upon this narrow trail. See, mine have long ago worn." The woman poked her foot out from beneath her gown; her foot was crammed into a spiked shod which glittered garishly. Gossamer's attention was drawn, instead, to the blue gown the woman wore beneath the patched cloak. It was of a rich weave, but appeared to be stained dark and stiff near the edges. The child's eyes traveled up the sleeve of the woman's arm. The sleeve also was stained dark and stiff, and deeply red. The child recoiled from the woman's grasp and began to struggle to break free. Her eyes sent plea full into the face of Paracoeur, who marched silently behind them.

He answered her. "Peace child. Remember, I bear the sword which Mistress Rachel fears."

"He, who lives by the sword, dies by the sword." Mistress Rachel mocked in a trembling, whine of a voice.

"Thou hast ken, Rachel, that Death hast not a claim to me or the Good King."

"Hence, it is that cowards sport with dangerous toys when they risk not," the woman's mocking voice grew bolder.

Paracoeur snorted and tightened his grip on his sword's hilt. "Thy friend, Death, is not a respecter of persons, wouldst thou profane him, as well, Mistress?

"Nay, Death has been a constant companion who refuses to grant boon to me. I am sly with those from whom I court favor." The beautiful woman's face began to furrow as a field plowed by untamed oxen. Of a sudden, she loosed Gossamer's hand and buried her face in her own aging hands.

"Oh, woe is me! My children...my children snatched from my arms and dashed to pieces." Heart- wrenching sobs wracked the woman's body which began to shrivel and shrink right before Gossamer's eyes.

The Gossamer was moved with compassion, no longer repelled by the woman's stained garb, she knelt and held the woman's head to her own chest, patting her back as if the crone were a nursling. "There, Dear Woman, do not weep so. Take comfort that the King is good and full of justice. He shall work his vengeance on those who have wronged thee."

"Nay, child...he shall not. It is he who has afflicted me to punish me for my indiscretions.... Spiteful,

spiteful being- he has left me to the wolves and famine…." The wrinkled woman began to shriek in a shrill voice.

Gossamer covered her own ears and began to shrink away looking to Paracoeur, at once with eyes of fear and accusation. Could it be the woman spoke with vert? Was the King harshly unforgiving and cruel in recompense? Gossamer's heart puzzled and was courted by great dread. Heavy in heart, she sat down on trail's edge and watched her two companions.

With voice solemn and full of pronouncement, Paracoeur answered the woman's accusations: "There hast naught come upon thee, that thou wert not warned concerning. And never hast the hands of mercy been neglected towards thee. The King's heart longs for restoration, but thou hast snubbed his offers ...and beleaguered and slain his messengers. "

"Ah, that… a mere misunderstanding on my part." The Mistress Rachel rose and stood erect, wiping her face upon her blood stained sleeve and smoothing her gown.

"Thou hast preferred thine blood-stained raiment, thou wanderest with eyes downcast, wearing out shods and spewing lies." Paracoeur continued in a steady voice.

"I do not lie!" The woman turned haughty eyes toward the King's liege. "I speak the vert writ in the King's own hand."

"Nay, dear, dear Rachel, the bitterness rooted in beater hath corrupted thy ken and blinded thy whole self. Come, I have boon and comfort to offer to thee in the Good King's name: The King would forgive and woo thee, yet once again, Mistress Rachel for he hast always cherished thee." Paracoeur took his hand from the sword hilt and extended it to the woman.

Rachel rose even more erect and stretched out her hand, palm vertical and toward him; instead of clasping the hand of Paracoeur, she rasped in a dark and unlovely tone. "Stay far from me, it is thou who hast darkened understanding. I will not be unfaithful to my kingly suitor again. Thou art correct; the suffering has been my penance for the foolishness of youth. Thou dost not grasp that I must wait and obey the writ of his own hand until he comes in triumph for me."

"Dear Woman, be reasonable." Paracoeur pleaded. "Thou kennest that the King hath come to thee, and thou hast rebuffed him cruelly."

"Nay, I have never met him on this trail. Never once hast he rode in triumph and shining armor on these trails. I would ken such. The King, he is comely beyond compare; full of grace and might…." The Woman slowly turned away from the King's Liege, all the while pulling the hood of her cloak up over her tresses until it covered her face. She began to amble down the wide path murmuring the King's praises to her own self, as if they were a charm.

Paracoeur released a deep and painful sigh and offered his outstretched hand to Gossamer. "Come, Child, it is well to return to our narrow path. "

Yet, as the skirt of the woman scarce disappeared beyond the trail bend, a mighty shaking trembled the earth. The King's liege thrust the young maid behind his own self, raised his great golden shield and held his unsheathed sword, flashing high above his head. "Foot thee, Gossamer… to the woods, I shall bid aide come to thee and remove thee from this cursed trail…."

The Gossamer, however, stood as if wholly earth-rooted, doe-eyes wide and stunned afeard; for straightway, a tremendous beast came crashing through the broad leafed bosk, turning it askew as if it were mere brush. A creature of enormous size with scales at once like cold blue-steel, but also fluid–red, like flame; its gape was wide and needle teethed, its dagger-shaped eyes sluiced with bile and a stomach -wrenching reek poured from its gape like a squall. Its great clawed feet struck the ground with force and speed and it began to advance on Paracoeur with its red glaring eye fastened upon the fragile Gossamer.

"Sssstand asssssside, I would sssup on thy tender trifle, Liege." The creature hissed and then thundered a roar that rattled leaves from the trees until the trees stood bare-branched. Its breath scorched the trail before him, but did not warm the shods of the Paracoeur, who called once more to the Gossamer.

"Up with thy shield, Young Maid, and flee, as I have told thee. Obey thy instruction, enton swiftly!" He commanded her and began to charge helm bent on, like an armored battle steed, toward the advancing dragon.

The voice of Paracoeur seized her ear and the Gossamer was roused from her stun; she reached for her shield and held it before her. Alas, it was no larger than a platter and her fear was shrinking it rapidly. She could feel the dragon's breath around its edges. Of a sudden, the very foundation of the travel-hardened trail was torn asunder and the earth opened his gape to swallow her whole, but the violent quake threw her leeward to crash against the splintered trunk of a stride- wide awl. Gossamer tried to grip the trunk shards and steady her footing, but she was thrown aside when the earth bellowed its gape anew.

The air was choked with caustic vapors and she scarce could see the combatants. Above the deafening crack of trees uprooted and branches ripped in twain she heard the vociferous snarls of the scaled dragon:

"Thy ssshods dare not find hearth on this path I prowl. Why tempteth thou evident doom? I ssshalt ssswallow thy charge, Liege of the Farmer King!" Its scythe claw gashed the earth, grave-deep.

No bosk bawl muted the Paracoeur's reply: "Take flight, Wyrm, thou art no match for this blade! It sings to feast on serpent flesh. It shall slake its thirst on thy life's ooze before the noct nods thrice." The Gossamer's champion loomed large before the steaming beast, the acrid smoke dared not trouble his gleaming silver eyes, but blew back from Paracoeur to its source, causing the monster's dagger eyes to sluice, even more. The bronzed visage of Paracoeur was sternly calm as he thrust his weapon at the dragon's throat. The clash of wrought weapon against the beast's iron like scales clanged like a gong, splitting rocks with its tenor. The sting of singing sword upon smoking scale reverberated through the Gossamer's dwindling shield and burrowed to her bone until she tremored like the very earth she sought to stand upon.

"Perssuaded thou art of thy own might. It ssslips thy mind, then, that I am ssly and insssiduous. Bring on thy lance, if thou daressst; it ssshall sssnap like a sapling of a bored awl.

"Nay, Foe. Thy sinister wit is mere sport akin the King's Name. Flee whilst thou hast breath to seethe."

The sky was sodden black with a stench that strangled her nost as the young maid struggled to bring herself to foot. Again the spar of sword arc sparked from the serpentine body armor that swirled with molten glow. And a screeching howl greeted the sword's embrace.

"Ho, Gossamer, heed thee to height before thine own flesh boils in this cauldron heat." Her protector, Paracoeur, shouted just as the child fled in full panic off trail, crashing into bare-branched trees. She ran, full-out, until she tripped upon a stone and fell sprawling. Her face skidded into cinders and acrid- smelling char. She began to choke, having swallowed some of the cindered soil and staggered about on quaking earth to regain her stance. Of a sudden, her frock was seized from behind and she found herself rising. Dizzied from tumult, the maid was lifted high above the bosk; rising goodspeed above the battle.

She ascended above the bosk; the span of such was far scorched like a feral flame's unquenched crave. Below the crush of battle clamored, and Dragon thundered a warning… "Thou ken that thou exceedeth the King's appointed era. Back down Liege, lest thou win his disfavor."

"Cease thy deceit , Wyrm and preparest thou for just assault . It is thee who trespass the decrees, ken thou that the Son's promised is bane to thy rumbler." And the defender's two edged blade answered the denizen's warning by biting through its iron- sheathing. A howl splintered the dark clouds and a shaft of light speared through the whorl of smog to shine upon the sword, which far exceeded its former breadth and flashed golden pure.

.

The Gossamer trembled anew at such sights and squirmed to see that which lifted her high above the fray. Straining to look up, she saw the barred silver wings of an immense, feathered Peregrine- the span of which was ten strides wide. Without warning, the sky flashed with a great lightening and Gossamer heard a shriek that shattered the blue air ashard. Looking down toward the earth, which was receding at a fast pace, she saw the Dragon had recoiled from the sword's arc, his great clawed legs chewed up the trail in flight from Paracoeur till naught but the dragon's howls hung echoing in the acid-etched air…

"Be thou warned, Liege…sssomeday, I will to catch the minikin without thy sssword nearby. " The dragon stopped mid flight and turned at ease: "Ssseeth now, thou hast chased away my appetite for triflings…I musssssst needsss go have ssssome sssport with the King's discarded ssstrumpet. SSShe giveth me quite a chassse, but I alwaysss tear at her heelssss"

At that very brief, Gossamer's rumbler lurched. Her winged carrier banked left and lofted high above the very expansive wilderness. The immense Peregrine swiftened its wings and the maid fell faint, afeard.

*　　　　　　　　*　　　　　　　　*

Almost a Coeur d'Luz pass later, Gossamer awoke. Perhaps it was the feathers that tickled her nost. She began to sneeze and at once opened her eyes to find herself in a colossal nest. Nearby, some very ugly nestlings were striving for a big stride- lengthed shiner that dangled from the curved beak of the immense she-peregrine. The young maid scrambled and tucked her feet and arms beneath her white woven cloak, pulling its hood snug over her crowned head until she was like unto a small egg tucked under the rim of the nest. There were feathers everywhere- sticks ...or were they small trees? The nest was littered with bird dung and food scraps. She wrinkled her nost in disgust. The silver headed she bird looked directly at Gossamer and winked a platter-sized eye in the girl's direction. Gossamer was unsure whether to wink back or hide, lest she be fed to the squawking nestlings. She decided a quick smile would be wise and then hunkered down even further and pulled her hood down over her face. Despite the putrid odor and the incessant squawking, the maid soon surrendered to an exhausted, dreamless sleep.

Gossamer awoke to a lavender sky and the sound of scraping near her left ear. She peered out from under her hood in time to see Paracoeur scale the edge of the giant nest and drop expertly at her feet.

"Methinks, thou hast lodged my charge, a night in thy Inn." He chuckled, "A bit unkempt, but verily thou art an opportune and clement hostess."

The Young maid breathed a sigh of relief, no longer afeard of becoming bird sup. She leaped up and ran full on into his breastplate, burying her nost in the sleeve of his tunic. Of a wonder, she marveled that the stench of battle and smoke did not linger on his garb. He smelled, as always of rosemary.

Paracoeur laughed and hugged his charge soundly in greeting. The immense Peregrine flew to a rocky ledge near the nest. And the King's liege waved his hand in salutation: "Faithful friend, how fleet thou art in flight. Thank thee for thy hospitality. May the King reward thee for thy boon to us."

The weather did not hold. Soon, lightening clawed at the ridge, which shadowed the field. The Stranger stood upright and alone in the center of the village's field; while an angry, howling wind pummeled him from all sides. Gasping through the dark clouds, the moon fought back against the surly wind that threatened to smother the breath from its round, innocent face. The field was half planted. Night stormed like a jealous mate and yet the Stranger toiled.

As he bent to drop a seed and smoothed the soft loam over it, he saw again the broken hearth of Old Simeon. Unwilling to forsake the field, the promise of harvest ever before him, the Stranger remained. The storm could rage; he would plant on.

Dropping another seed into a hole poked by the cane, he thought of Anna who trusted him with what little she had. He knew that the hope of the village rode on his shoulders this night. As long as he had strength within him, he would plant.

He remembered the fevered rage of the village official, whose body was bound with plague and dropped another row of precious seed, struggling against the violent winds.

He could not do otherwise. He had no choice. Compassion stirred him. The village harlot had wept at his feet. Honor requested his faithfulness. He stabbed the rain-swelled loam with his cane and dropped another seed.

The Stranger's ears were deaf to the shrieks of the wind. Instead he heard again the cloaked elder who had whispered: "And I have seed which cries for a field. It will never find its way there upon my feeble back." Even though his own back ached, the Stranger labored on. He was unwilling that any in the village should perish from hunger come the Barebranch past next. Indeed, though troubled greatly, he still shouldered the poke of seed. For, he knew the heart of the King and had pledged himself to it.

The air was tight. Like a stiff parchment it wrapped them with empty heat. The sharp and pungent scent of sage pricked their nosts. Gossamer made a shallow sigh. She longed for the deeply green bosk where every breath was full and pregnant with growth. She was dry and cotton-mouthed and she was not in the mood to sing. Staring at the pale, cloud-barren sky, the dull thud of her beater was as monotonous as the desolate landscape. Freed from the trance-like numbness by the faint whisper of jingles, she slowly turned her blank stare toward Paracoeur and mused upon her companion. As customary, he rested with hands ever diligent; hindered neither by clime nor circumstance. He had settled upon that flat, red rock as if it were a throne.

Indeed, the brawny, silver-haired knight was bent over weave, closely examining the seam he had presently tailored. "Young Maid,' he said. "Come, make haste behind yon rock and try the fit." He nodded towards a large steed-sized stone.

She was loathe to rise in the heat and voiced: "Old Knight, Of a favor, leave be till noctide. This stone plain holdeth heat like an ola!

"Thy frock hath shrunk upon thy lengthening limbs till it is naught but a shrift. Quicken thyself in all haste, Maid," he paused, glancing northward. "Methinks, we best advance well before noctide.

Listlessly, Gossamer rose and crossed the stride of crusted sandstone that crunched beneath her feet. Her cloak was swathed about her in the style of a desert dweller and the constant dry wind whipped the cloak's hem at her feet.

"Paracoeur, I shalt fair bake inside this helm. Verily, there is naught lurking about with a quiver full. I would remove it and breathe cooler."

"Stay thy protests, Maid, the helm is needed. Now hie thee behind that rock."

And she went, though reluctantly. The rock formation sheltered her in shade large enough to protect her from sun's scorch. She exchanged her shrift for the new garment, unhurriedly. Then, squinting against the glare, she stepped out from behind the rock to twirl before the King's Liege.

"A fine fit." He pronounced with a grin, all the while his wise eyes weighed her growth. His charge had sprouted from the fragile child to a young woman, willowy in grace; the shape of her filled the just-sewn garment with a delicate balance. She had once been near to his knee and enton stood a handspan above his arm's crook.

"Now, thou lackest solely a few things."

"Only a few?" She playfully replied, tossing her cream-colored curls till they danced like a cascade of vanilla fleurs in the wind. Her translucent skin was pinked at the cheeks.

. "Aye, a few… don thy cloak and helm. Thou must gird thy cloak with a girdle against capricious winds." He said and pulled a brilliant belt out of his ever-present poke.

She fetched her constant garb and stood ready to receive the bequest. "Old Knight, it is of a vert, pure beauty." She lowered her chin before Paracoeur. Crafted, as it was of the three finger thick chains of highest quality gold, silver and copper, fired and plunged, that were linked together intricately, the belt was exquisitely designed. The desert sun reflected from the gleaming girdle in myriad directions.

"Beautiful and necessary; every warrior must needs tie up the ends of their cloak to be fleet in pursuit.'

"Old Knight," she said fondly. "I be a maiden promised to the Royal Heir, not a warrior."

"Hath thou armor?" he queried.

"Some."

"Believe that I spoke verily when I early warned of arduous journey. If thou wouldst consent to be the Son's Bride, thou must become a warrior."

"Thou art always brooding!" She playfully chided. "Methinks thou seekest to present me to thy King fully garbed as one of thy own guild.

"Ah...," Paracoeur sat upon the rock, his hand stroking his beard. "Let it be so...as if we be of one blood and kin."

Gossamer gazed at her companion and counselor. Puzzled more often than not by his remarks, she had grown tall walking beside him. Even on a sunpass such as this, a view-full of Paracoeur would calm her soul and tune her beater.

"Fair Nursemaid," she bowed low before him with a giggle in her voice, "hast thou anymore fashionable garb for thyr charge?"

"Aye," his huge, scarred hand plunged once more into his murex poke and pulled from its thong-gathered gape, a breastplate. Centered of pure gold, it was circled with leaves of hammered brass - a perfect fit for the maiden. "Step forward and I will clasp thou within this buckler's grasp." He said as he fastened the fire-forged buckles to embrace her cloak-draped shoulders.

"How is it that poke holds boons of such a size?"

"I have my mysteries, thou knowest."

"...it is too much weight! I've not the strength to sport thy fashion."

Paracoeur grinned with lighted eyes, drew his great sword and lightly tapped Gossamer's calves. "Be quickened in strength, willow limbs!" He commanded.

Clapping in delight, she squealed. "Three boons thou givest in a single pass of Coeur d'Luz! Thy generosity abounds legend, Old Knight!" Hastily, however, her face clouded over and her lips formed into a pout. "Methinks thy. cedar trunk arms grow too tired to carry me when I grow weary."

Laughter erupted from the depths of his rumbler. Throwing his King's cloak back over his shoulders, he flexed his bronzed arms until they bulged like the legs of chariot pullers. "Think again!" He raucously roared, plucking her from the desert floor as one would pluck a meadow fleur; he tossed her like a feather, high into the wind. She could scarcely breathe from laughing. Paracoeur continued to toss her as deep, rolling waves of laughter echoed about the arid, rocky landscape like the crash of storm-drenched ocean waves. Then, ever mindful of her ivory skin, he sprinkled water from his copper flask upon her brow. With a playful slap, he shut her helm's visor and set her down.

"Even a porcelain trinket needs to stand on its own, Young maid." He chided in jest

Gossamer's peals of laughter faded away in ever widening echoes and she looked down at her own two feet. She had long ago stretched the lamb mocs which the skilled knight had crafted. Now, her feet stood firm in bronze shods, akin to those of Paracoeur.

She stood resplendent and looked straight into Coeur d'Luz.

Remembering that Noct's pass long before when the then small child had shrunk accusingly from the Dawn's light, the King's Liege regarded the Young maid with satisfaction:

"Hither, once again, to journey we go. There is a crowned city not far from here. It is time thou wert schooled in her scrolls."

Cinnamon-hued rocks which had been wind swept into billowing sculptures of cloud shapes ordered one edge of the desert wash they now traversed. Opposite, the lightening and wind had conspired to chisel and hammer spires upon the sun-baked anvil of the desert flats. In concert, they had crafted angularly-shaped rock shards, deep rust in color, that towered over the desert floor casting long knife- shaped shadows far east out into the wastelands.

Paracoeur paused in his tread and sniffed the air. Nodding, he began to hum a faint melody and walked on. Soon the young maid joined her hum to his.

The Coeur d'Luz had made his journey until he hung in the western sky. His golden hue was less severe than at altpass. Small strands of cooler evening air began to weft through the tapestry of blistering heat. Gossamer thought to herself that she would welcome the noct with a grateful nod. Directly ahead, thrice-creamed java colored columns unevenly lined a high mesa which drifted lazily in and out of view. She heard again the faint, melodic tones of jingles floating from high atop the mesa.

White mineralized dust lay in patches along the sinuous edges of a shallow, sand colored river that snaked at a sluggish pace through the lowest points of the desert wash. The air was motionless above the river, which was deep enough only to wet the sole of a shod. The river puddled opportunely here and there becoming like a glaze upon the sand.

Once again, the trusted liege quieted his shods, turned his ears to the north and listening intently.

This time, he addressed Gossamer with urgency in his deep voice: "It is now wise to quicken our pace. We need to climb yon high mesa."

"Ah, Liege, every time the journey would begin to ease, must thou devise some new and arduous task? Look! The air begins to cool and, see, a trace of droplets begin to refresh this poor parched river."

At that moment, the air thickened and grew heavy with rain-scent. Gossamer heard the staccato of tiny drops hit her helm and she smiled as the droplets formed a veiled mist that brushed lightly against her rose pinked cheeks.

"Nay, Lass. Gird up thy cloak and quicken thy pace. Listen! Dost thou not hear the low drone afar off?

"But, Counselor, it is only beginning to rain…and I am as athirst as this land."

"Run with me! We must outstrip the wild wind. A wash is not a place of safety when the desert skies weep. There is little time! Run with me, to the shelter of the high rock mesa. That wind drives a wall of ag before it."

As they ran, the afar off drone growled itself into an angry roar. Paracoeur grabbed Gossamer's arm and together they sped, the wind pounding on their backs with a great fury. They reached the foot of the high rock mesa and began to scramble up its storm-pocked base. The roar intensified in their footsteps.

Climbing hard and fast they reached a sandstone ledge that was ringed with swollen, spiny plants. Paracoeur reached for the next cleft in the rock to pull them higher but a gnawing curiosity caused Gossamer to fight his firm grasp. She turned just as lightening blazed its fiery veins across the sky.

The sight she saw nailed her shods to the ledge. A wall of rushing tormented, grime-colored ag, at least forty hand spans high, charged toward them. Like a many-horned stag in rut fever it upturned skeleton tress and gored the rock borders of the now engorged wash. In an instant the tossing, tormented ag beast seized at her shods and swept her along with them as it thrashed further down the mesa-bordered gulch.

The swirling, tumultuous flood beast battered her against everything in its path; pushing and pulling her in every direction at once. She thrashed about wildly and fought to capture breath for her straining lungs, but the weight of her own armor aided the ag in dragging her deep into the swollen torrents. Energized by sheer panic, she managed to briefly surface for a gulp of fresh air.

Above the ag's near defeating roar, she heard Paracoeur's clear call:

"Fear thee not, I am here. Take thy shield in hand."

A flash of disbelief swam through the torrents of fear and confusion in her head. "The shield is too heavy, too small...but..." she thought. She heard again the voice of her companion calling her name and then she thrust her hand through the thrashing ag and laid hold of her shield; the thong of which was, at that moment, strangling her about the neck. The raging ag began to twist itself into a cyclone shape. She struggled to lift the shield above the force of the ag. Instead she felt herself lifted from the plunging, twisting waters.

She awoke retching and choking. Paracoeur was kneeling beside her and gently turned her on her side so the swallowed ag could be pumped like bilge from her rumbler. She was bruised and lay limply, a mere speck on the wide expanse of the mesa top. Her eyes were shut and her breast heaved, even yet in breath struggle. Some time passed before she again ventured to open her eyes. Her exhausted gaze was met by that of her protector, Paracoeur, and she saw that she lay sheltered fully by his shadow. She smiled weakly. With a gentle touch, Paracoeur cupped her head in his great scarred palm.

Smiling back at her, he kindly chided: "Methinks thou shouldst surely learn to swim, before wading out too deep, Beloved of the King's Son." He wiped her face with the broidered edge of his white woven cloak. Then he gently removed her helm and breastplate, the weight of which had pinned her fatigued body to the sandy mesa top. Shifting slightly, Paracoeur allowed the sun to softly massage warmth into Gossamer's limbs. She surrendered to sleep's lullaby cooed by distant desert doves.

Once during the dusky blue noct, she awakened to see her friends from long ago, the stars, winking to her health. The noct air was filled with the rhythm of many drippings and occasionally the sounding tinkle of jingles, coming ever nearer. The desert noct breeze blew its fragrantly cool breath over her skin and soothed her, at last, into a deep slumber.

When Dawn began her dance across the eastern sky, the maiden arose to greet her, refreshed and strengthened. She sensed that Paracoeur hovered near about, at scout perhaps, and she was satisfied that he would return at the right time, or sooner should she call.

From below the cliffs, the sounds of splashing and low bleating drifted up accompanied by a lively chant chimed by many jingles. Gossamer's curiosity was piqued. However, before leaving her noct nest on the great white woven cloak, she donned her garb and stared bravely into the brightening Dawn. When suitably dressed, she flew Paracoeur's cloak in the breeze to cleanse it from sand and carefully folded and placed it on a rock to await his return.

Shyly she crept toward the cliff's edge and peered below. A cacophonous carnival of sight and sound enticed her. To her surprise, the angry ag had settled beneath the cliffs into a placid reddish pool of about thirty strides across. All around the tamed pool, white, wooly creatures lapped, with tin jingles hung from their brightly ribboned collars. To Gossamer's increasing wonder, young maidens, dressed in homespun skirts hiked up in their hands with hems dripping, waded in the shallows of the ruddy pool. The sound of their laughter and playful splashing piped an invitation to the Gossamer. The servant girls gamboled in the dirty pond and began to toss an object between them. Again curious, Gossamer rose to her feet for a better look.

Shrieks echoed wildly from below, as the shepherdesses pointed upward and fled to the pond's edge. The Dawn had thrown aside her gauzy morning veil and rose in splendor behind Gossamer, whose helm reflected the bright rays.

Below the cliff, the maids were at once afraid and amazed. For the Coeur d'Luz's light danced over Gossamer's sparkling white cloak and vanilla curls and made her appear as if she were a kin to the Great Coeur d'Luz. Immediately, the peasant girls fell to their knees, pressing their faces into the damp sandy shore. A wordless droning arose from the canyon floor, accompanied by athe jarring dissonance of bleats and tin jingles. The wooly creatures became jittery and rushed in-group to pack themselves into an ag-gouged nook in the rock canyon wall.

Gossamer felt a steady hand on her shoulder and Paracoeur's voice stated: "They are afeared."

"Afeared of what?"

"Afeard of thee, the brightness of thy armor pierces their darkness. Come; let us be on our way. The citadel we seek lies there," he pointed northward. "It is a good pass of Coeur d'Luz' trek from here."

Across the tableau of the high mesa, another mesa stretched higher and farther still. "Another wilderness to cross...another mesa to trap a raging storm..." Gossamer was reluctant to consider the expanse, remembering her trial in ag. She turned her gaze below. "I did not mean to frighten, but to greet. Perhaps I should climb down and show yon maidens that it is just I, and of a vert, the brightness reflects from the shods I walk in and the garb I wear."

Paracoeur considered and stated. "Tis always well to introduce the King's cloak to strangers. Go! Be mindful, though, our journey beckons."

Rapidly, Gossamer scaled down the canyon wall and ran to greet the maidens who shrank from her approach until they huddled, backed against the pool.

"Greetings," she called.

Again afeared, they fell upon their faces. One cried out: "it is the terrible warrior goddess come to thieve us of our master's flocks!" and each maiden began to moan and weep.

"Nay," she called, "it is but I, a mere gossamer, dressed in protective garb. Thee hast mistaken me for the daughter of the Coeur d'Luz. Come, see. I do not burn."

The shepherdesses lifted their heads hesitantly, lifted themselves slowly to their own feet and began to edge forward. Little by little, chatter arose. "Look, she is beautiful...our master would desire her.... extraordinary beauty."

"Her eyes are peculiar....Her skin is palest, scraped ivory. She is comely above many ..."

"Look, her shods! The desert rocks will not trouble her feet...."

"She must be of a distant kingdom, such peculiar armor she wears..."

A shepherdess, more bold than the others who twittered behind her, stepped forward and began to stroke Gossamer's flaxen hair. The shepherdess was swarthy in complexion, with noct-dark eyes. Her hair was earth-colored, still dripping with pond water. There was a single gold hoop in one of her ears.

"Fair lady," the bold shepherdess spoke, " ye are far elegant and do not wear the garb of a desert dweller."

"Aye, I am from Nunatok high meadow ajourney to the home castle of the Great and Good King. '

Another peasant maiden stepped forward and began to finger the buckles of Gossamer's breastplate. "It is cool there, I have heard. Ye have journeyed far, then."

"Aye," Gossamer sighed, "and I am weary of this barren wasteland."

"So are we! " Another added, bending to peer closely at Gossamer's shods. "These art finely crafted. Weight a burden?"

"After a while, thee would not notice the weight of them. Here," Gossamer bent to remove her shod, "would thee like to try their fit?"

Instantly the six shepherdesses clamored around Gossamer eager to try the shods, and any other garb that she was willing to offer.

Some briefs later, Gossamer sat at pond's edge her legs stretched pale upon the sand. Several of the six maidens busied themselves plaiting her flaxen hair. Her garb was scattered along the shore, where those trying it had dropped it. The rest of the six, stripped to their underpinnings, languidly swam in the ruddy pond.

blue cord

When the hacking fits had subsided and the village elders had awakened from their exhausted stupor, they found themselves propped against all manner of things. Necks were stiff, and bodies twisted in discomfort, but no one had the strength to move at the brief. Some had fallen on the crumbling floor stones and slept where they had fallen. Some did not awake, at all. While the bodies of the village elders lay still and heavy with grogginess, their beaters did not. The smoldering coals of anger hearthed in their beaters, though covered with sleep's ash, glowed crimson. Brief by brief, the coals burnt through the fog of grogginess and heated their breasts with rage, once again.

A voice cracked the silence. "We must contain the Stranger. He must not trespass our field."

"And which of us could restrain him? His back is strong, his hands huge." A tired voice scorned.

"It is fact, we cannot even force our own feet to the field."

"If he plants and the field grows, the village will entreat him to stay. They will be wooed by the stranger…and for what purpose?" Another reasoned.

Someone snorted. "Ye fools, the field will not grow overnight. The plague will grow before the field does."

"Ye speak nonsense." Cai, the official, admonished sarcastically. "Always ye hath been one to greet the promise of Coeur d'Luz so cheerfully. We will not all perish. Some of us have hoarded grain just for such a time as this."

"I've no appetite. The fever clutches at my rumbler and threatens to wrench it from mine frame and thou speakest of hoarded grain? Two of my wee ones have ceased breath struggle. Thou art bereft of reason! " The Harbinger growled back.

"Take yer ease, the plague will pass. Plagues always do." Cai continued "This isn't the first I've seen."

"But many in our village have died and more will; some of us, perhaps," another voice chided.

"Perhaps so, then there will be a few less mouths to feed. The strong, the powerful will survive." The pock-faced Cai labored to stand, leaning heavily against his cane.

The grey and peeling door creaked open and another entered, hooded and bent.

"Ah, Nico, didst thou slumber the night in thine own hut?" The Official gestured a wide sweep to those in the chamber. "See, what didst I tell thee? The plague will pass and there will be those who survive."

Nico returned the Official's greeting with a wave of his own. "Indeed, it was the sweetest night I have spent in many, but what is abuzz in this room? Before I reached the door, voices swarmed around me like hornets."

"We are addressing what to do about the Stranger; or rather, he is." The Harbinger spoke as he daubed at his bandaged feet. "Those of us who are practical in nature have been silenced with sarcasm, or perhaps it is hope? My ears cannot weigh the difference any more."

"Such a sparkle of fresh water, ye art Harbinger," Cai brushed aside the comment and bent toward Nico. "We are attending to our duties of protecting the village from usurpers and ne'er-do-wells."

"Cai," the hooded Nico carefully chose his words. "Perhaps, our remaining strength would be better spent protecting our villagers from the plague that ravishes. Thou hast not been abroad in our streets. Desolation and despair walk freely there. There are few doorways that grief does not loiter in."

"Ye kenest, Nico, that the village poor can never be expected to hoard their vision. During hard times and good, they are caught in the web of daily need. They rely on we, who travel fleetly over that web, to lead them from the spider. Would ye have us abdicate our duties? We have a responsibility to protect those who can not protect themselves." Cai whispered fervently.

"I mean no disrespect, Old Friend, but I fear I hear the fever talking through yer usually adroit mouth. Look at yer own feet; they are bundled in pus-soaked rags. Ye canst not walk across the room, let alone navigate fleetly across a web. Yer horde of grain is useless, if ye canst not keep it down."

"A slight hindrance, it will pass, no doubt." Cai waved away Nico's comment as if it were a gnat.

"Thou art lame, Cai, and thou shouldst have let the Stranger tend to yer wounds."

"He is a stranger and unschooled in our ways. He would only do me harm." Cai shook his head resolutely.

"I think not."

"Ah," up spoke the Harbinger, who made a great mockery of scratching his coifed head. "And that is, after all, yer problem."

"I think… ye considereth the Stranger as a hunting spider. His back is strong. Ours are not. Even should the plague pass…the field will not produce grain for Barebranch past next, if it is not planted now." Nico looked each village elder in the eye. "Which of ye feels as if ye could carry one seed to the field?"

Some looked away, others groaned, but the coals in their heart grew no dimmer.

The Official, Cai, laughed a raspy note: "Ye hast lost the point, my Faithful Friend. I find the Stranger to have no more legs than I, and less ken of this village. The tenets were written to protect the village and those in power. His back art indeed stronger and he doth stand on healthy feet, no doubt. Should he plant in the field? I've no quarrel with feeding the villagers. I might add that one ox is as good as another."

Nico lowered his voice. "Then, why treateth him shamefully?"

"Ye wouldst choose hospitality over wisdom?"

"Following the King's decree art wisdom," Nico protested.

Cai leaned his head closer to that of Nico's and continued. "Of a vert, yea, but it is not always expedient. It is foolishness, in this instance, to ply the stranger with kindness when he seeks to favor the people from their duly appointed protectors." Murmuring voices had begun to cloud the room and Cai had raised his voice just enough to push his words at Nico.

"Ye unjustly givest motive to a man with a strong back and a compassionate soul. He doth not…" Nico had been whispering urgently to be heard by Cai only, but found it necessary to raise his voice to be heard above the increase of heated discussion, "intend to harm the people."

"I also think so. It is clear he threatens our existence," a voice, hot and excited, interrupted Nico's defense of the Stranger.

Like the stormy front of ag that heralds a flood, the voices rose in fervor and panic. Chaos filled the chamber. Reason was thrown against the chamber walls and crumpled to the floor; unheeded in the commotion.

Mid storm, Cai grabbed at Nico's ear and pulled it close, filling it with his hot, rank breath: " Ye hath misjudged me, my old, but weakened friend. I am not fevered but wise. I hate not the man, but he will move the village with his kindness and our power will perish. I repeat. Let him use his strong back like an ox, but let him not harvest what is rightfully ours."

At that, Nico cradled his own head in his arms and leaned heavily against the wall so that he could remain upright, since he no longer held a cane. The room was awash with the cries of a mob. Nico had looked directly into the eyes of the Official, his old but fevered friend, and saw not one hint of kindness there. He felt his way along the wall and left the chamber, unnoticed by all except Cai, who shook his head and glared after his weakened acquaintance.

Cai turned and intently scrutinized those left ablaze in the chamber, his stiff fingers traveled towards the velvet poke which hung from his richly carved belt. "Here!" He called the mob to his control. "I haven't much, but I will contribute this silver. Ye are correct, gentlemen. We are not strong enough to lay hold of the Stranger ourselves. But our silver can purchase the protection of the village."

Caught by the gleam of silver coins, the elders paused in their clamor and regarded the glint of Cai's highly polished teeth.

"Thirty pieces of silver will purchase an expedient solution. What other will contribute to the cause?"

Silence, like the humid lull before a raging whirlwind, filled the room for a pregnant, brooding brief; but, then a shower of silver coins clanked into the chamber's center.

Cai's pock-marked face grimaced into a broad grin as he motioned for a younger council member to retrieve the coins. Then he hobbled to the grey and peeling council door and mustered all his remaining strength to throw it wide open. In doing so, he fell from his perch upon his cane and face down in the muddy pool just outside the door.

red cord

Shrieking trumpets blared and split the air before the dungeon's gape. In less than a brief, the battle on the dungeon steps came to a halt. The flint-covered guards dropped their swords to their sides and stood as if on a parade ground. The lone, golden knight paused, as well.

A voice, cold and harshly rigid, assaulted the ears of she who lay bound by chains in the dust of the dungeon floor. "Thy battle is in vain. Kenest thou well that a broken bled covenant must be paid for in full. Justice demands death. Thou hast no legal right to descend bronze shod into the dungeon of this city. The law of the King must be satisfied, even here.

The dungeon was eerily silent from the absence of clash and clamor. Briefs stretched long, but she did not falter in her watch. The tension in the air grew ominously heavy and seemed to press upon her from all sides; it was much heavier than the iron chains. As though carved from stone and standing upon a game board, the warriors stood poised for orders.

With a steady hand, the lone, golden warrior laid the great, double-edged sword down upon the landing. To her amazement, he next removed his armor, as well. He turned and looked down the stairs; he looked full on into her eyes. Up until his grey-eyed glance met hers, she had not ken'd that he ken'd of her presence. The great, unclad warrior then turned his face into the streaming luz and bowed his head, standing vulnerably before the flint black guards.

Straightway, the guards broke rank, drew their flint daggers and as a mob fell upon the stripped warrior. To her greater amazement, the mighty warrior did not shield his brawny body from their blows.

Soon he fell to his knees and with his last breath uttered: "For Thine glory and thine beater, O King."

Then he fell motionless upon the landing, stretched beside the golden weapon that he had willingly laid down.

Most of the guards turned and marched methodically up the dungeon steps. One guard remained. He bent to peer closely at the fallen, golden champion. Swiftly, he pierced the side of the slain warrior. And from between the fallen defender's ribs sprang claret and ag which flowed freely from the wound. The blackened guard wiped his blade against his obsidian breast plate, turned and followed his squad up the stairs.

A mighty moan broke within she that lay in the dust. Her beater throbbed like a womb which struggles to push out a stillborn babe. Her lungs, energized with vigor from the wind she had breathed, issued a desolate wail which echoed incessantly through the yawning rock hewn cavern where she lay.

She would die soon. This she ken'd...She would die soon, of this she was sure. At the top of the dungeon stairs, the carved obsidian door had fallen almost shut. Only a single beam of light challenged the darkness which had rushed from the corners to reclaim the dungeon. The thin beam descended the stairs and shone upon the hilt of the great golden, double edged sword. Blood, like spilled burgundy wine, pooled inch deep along the landing and ran like ag to a ditch until it fell over the far edge onto the cold stone step below.

She would die soon. Her eyes grew weary and glazed as she lay in the dust and watched the blood drip from step to step. A steady rhythmic beat accompanied the dirge played by her beater.

The Stranger stooped low and watched the loam slip through his fingers as he gently covered the last seeds in the furrow. He breathed deeply of the warm, rain-scented earthy fragrance that wafted from the soil. He marveled at the wonder of the treasure held within the seeds: the timid green of first sprout, the plush carpet of vigorous growth, the burnished ocean of grain that would soon cast its waves in the sunlight, the winnowing fork sending the chaff a-flight, the thick walled adobe oven heated by cedar fire. Closing his eyes, he could see the plump barley loaves laid out in baskets on tables surrounded by hard working men, dove-eyed women and restless children. A smile spread across his dirt spattered, bearded face as he thought more: after the loaves were broken and the wine poured there would be lots of talk and laughter…How he loved to hear the squeals of delighted children!

He had labored through the night and the muscles in his back ached from stooping low over the furrows. The stranger patted the planted soil one last time, and gently wiped his hands against each other to clean the dirt from them. His hands were heavily calloused and huge, but his touch gentle enough to have planted each seed.

Leaning forward he began to put his weight on the walking stick so that he could rise from his stooped position, when his nosts twitched. The air suddenly grew thick with the sickly, sweet scent of pomade and sweat. The gentle eyes of the stranger widened slightly in recognition and he laid the walking stick down in the dirt before him. From the corner of his eye, he saw the unwashed, roughly-woven ruddy robes just before he felt the first club blow to his head. A rain of blows beat down on him while worn leather shods kicked his ribs. Blood dripped from the crown of his head into his eyes, just as he turned to behold his attackers. An unruly bunch of underfed thugs mobbed him from all sides hurling insults and fists, clubs and fierce kicks. The stranger smiled with blood stained teeth and whispered "and so it begins...hold it not to their account...dear Father; they are blinded by silver and empty rumblers."

When the ragged mob trudged away, cutting a swath over the freshly planted furrows, the stranger lay face down, thrown like refuse on a heap upon the last seeds that he had planted. The blood trickling from his crown joined a rivulet that dripped from between his ribs. A crimson pool began to puddle about the stranger's body until it met with a rain puddle that had pooled during the night between the rows.

Dawn stopped her dance in a brief and a drape of darkness seemed pulled across the sky. The stranger lay dead amongst the furrows in the blackened field.

Much time later, Nico stood with his hand held like a visor above his eyes from where he stood on the ridge above the village field. Brief by brief, the Coeur d'Luz sent his search throughout the earth, its scout rays causing the furrows to glitter. The weakened, hooded man leaned against the ox that was harnessed to a rough-hewn coal cart. When the Coeur d'Luz grew bold and threw its light heralds at the field, Nico slumped in sorrow. There below him in the field lay a body, bruised beyond recognition. Nico sighed deeply and gathered his courage as he led the ox down into the field. He noted how curiously the sun painted the rain-filled furrows rust red. From the ridge above, the entire field looked like a lake of blood.

Some time later, Nico had reached his goal. He knelt beside the stranger's battered, death-stiffened body and struggled with all his will to lift the stranger into the cart. Nico had promised himself to seek justice on the part of the stranger. From this moment on, Nico would no longer be welcome within the council chambers, this he knew. It was of no import any longer. Nico's soul was seared with the weight of sorrow and guilt and he was determined to bear the burden of it like the man he was. Against his own plague- weakened frame with a strength deeply willed, Nico braced the stranger and lifted him into the cart. The tears that streamed down Nico's face fell upon the stranger's bloodied hands and washed them clean.

Slowly the ox trudged down the trail that would lead to the highway which would lead to the King's outpost city. Nico held tightly to the side of the coal cart and was pulled along. One foot in front of another, he staggered under the weight that seemed to press down upon him.

Many a Coeur d'Luz pass later, Nico nodded awake when the ox snorted. Nico placed his weary hand upon the wheel of the cart and pulled himself into a stand. The air was scented heavily with rose petals and Nico's forehead wrinkled above his eyes. He glanced around and saw no gardens- just the barren landscape, edged with wisps of hardy grass that stretched before him on his journey. The stench of rotting death had enveloped the coal cart burdened with the stranger's body for the last two passes. Nico was clearly puzzled and turned to glance within the coal cart turned bier and found his puzzlement increase. The coal cart was empty; scrubbed clean, its birch sides fair sparkling.

Nico's face fell. He was indeed further disheartened; perhaps he had slept too soundly and thieves had come in the night to claim the stranger's body for their bounty. His plague-sapped body lost its remaining strength and he fell at the side of the road, sheltered from the harsh light of Dawn by only the cart's shadow.

Again, Nico was roused from his stupor sleep by the stamping of the ox, who grew impatient in harness. Nico glanced wearily down the road and pulled himself upright again. He struggled to climb into the cart and urged the ox down the road toward the Good King's outpost. Nico had promised himself to seek the King's face on the part of the stranger. And he was a man of his word.

red cord

The dripping blood became as a metronome and filled the dungeon with a ceaseless, slow beat; relieving her of the need to count her own breaths. She was not willing to surrender her vision to the dark void that beckoned her with increasing boldness. Though glazed with pain and shielded with stone grief, her eyes were trained on the rain of blood that descended from one worn stone step to the next. Even though the time was measured in beat, enton; it seemed like eons since the spear of luz had first pierced the black dungeon. Of a vert, she had not moved against the chains in so long that her body was numb and felt much like the cold, dust-covered stone she lay upon. Where the stone ended and her body began had long ceased to be distinguishable. Only the beater within her showed signs of life and that steadily tiring beater beat only once to every ten drips of the blood. The dripping was thrown in echoes round between the dungeon walls.

Did she think of the slain warrior who laid, still, some steps above? No, there were no thoughts in her throbbing brain. Only the sound of dripping, only the eyes trained upon the claret-colored drops that fell, one at a time, from the steps above. Her beater no longer ached with longing. A calm, much like the dead of night sat dull and heavy upon her breast as she awaited the end. She had surrendered to death's advance when she realized the warrior had fallen. She simply waited watching the color flow down the stairs with the passionless stare of an aged one who rocks back and forth, a face as stone cold as the tomb it faces.

Drip, drip drip… one. Drip, drip, drip, drip, drip….two. Drip.drip…. *How long? Oh, Death…thou taketh thy sweet time approaching.* Her own impatient thought startled her from the stupor that she lay in, too drunk with fate to struggle. Her eyes still eyed the crimson beads that fairly curtained the stone steps down into the dungeon but she had long ceased to be aware of the sight.

Until one drip sounded louder than the rest; as if it hammered upon her very ear drum. She summoned the strength to narrow her eyes and willed them to actually see. She was a bit surprised to find a bead of blood poised at the precipice of the step nearest her. A shard of luz, from the narrowed opening of the partially closed obsidian door, struck the step nearest to her and she watched the luz seemingly bring life to the dull, red bead of blood on the stair's edge. Caught between the beat of time, the blood drip oozed slowly over the stair edge and fell ever so slowly toward her lifeless hand that lay stretched, bone-thin like frost, close to the bottom of the steps. She gathered the will to think a thought and remembered how she had stretched with all her might toward the beam of approaching luz. Enton, she regarded the blood bead with a detached curiosity. Would it feel as cold as she or had the shard of luz warmed it?

purple cord

Silence hung between them like a heavy veil. Gossamer felt weighted down and grimy. As she walked, she kept her eyes to the ground, constantly aware of the tarnish on her breastplate and the dent in her shod. She had walked nearly four hours next to her companion,

Paracoeur, and had yet to speak one word to him. The Coeur d'Luz was unmercifully bearing down upon her and sweat stung at her eyes. The desert had been swallowed by waist -high shrubs; sparse evergreens that filled the air with a sharp, almost metallic bite.

"Gossamer?"

She held her hand out upright with palm turned out, intending to silence him. It was not a time for words. Her thoughts were filled with pictures… repulsive pictures of campfires and dancing …and charred flesh. She had no wish to bear his patronizing voice. She did not even turn her head to meet his gaze. It would be better if he walked ahead or behind…or better yet, out of her sight. The steady drumming of his march next to hers was a cadence of shame for her own shods which she sluggishly dragged across the dry, pale dirt. She was weary and worn with a weight which pressed upon her soul. Her armor was heavy and a burden she felt not fit to carry.

Here and there, a lark sang to her from its hiding place on a shrub bough. But her soul was too leaden to dance to its pipe. Overhead, carrion birds glided in long lazy circles. Their shadows silently passed over her, like rain clouds awaiting an appointed deluge. Out of the corner of her eye, she could see the bright glare of Paracoeur's white cloak. Her shield hung shrunken near the small of her back.

"Gossamer?"

"Please," her words stung out a reply. 'I do not want…I can not talk with thee."

"If thou canst not talk, trouble thyself but a little to listen." He calmly suggested.

"Leave me be….mine ears are full of jarring jingles…thy voice burdens me with its velvet. Thou kenest I am now coarse as the desert sand itself."

"I ken not…but that a bath in clean ag might do thee well. " He quietly replied.

"No bath will clean mine heart. I am common now; not fit for a king."

"Thou knowest not the King, if thou thinkest he is loathe to look upon the common."

"O Paracoeur," she dropped to her knees, which felt the coarse gravel keenly. "How can thee stay with me? I have become like the harlot we met on the trail; casting aside my cloak, my boons crafted from thine own hand?"

She remembered, now, vividly: how she had awakened, stretched out brazenly on the dung-fouled bank of a muddy puddle. Alone; her garb scattered about and half trampled into the sand. The peasant girls and their flocks had vanished. A thin acrid smoke curled up from charred lamb bones; all that remained from the noct's revel. She remembered looking fully into the face of Paracoeur where he sat, quietly on a rock, an arm's breadth from her. He had spread his cloak over her nakedness. On his shoulder was a lambkin, tiny and ruined by a trampling flock. She remembered the compassion in his deep eyes. And how she had sought to scramble up and almost fell when her head pounded painfully. She had quickly dressed, climbed the cliff wall and begun to walk determinedly forward on their journey, without nary a word.

Looking now at her hands, she noticed how her fingernails were blackened with sooty grease and tears began to traverse her stained face.

Of an instant, Paracoeur was at her shoulder. "There, there, Precious One…"he comforted his charge with soft words and gentle pats.

"Counselor, leave me be…I wish to soak in my sorrow. I have grievously trampled upon the King's favor. I am a ruined goss." She pushed him away.

"Thou seekest to sulk and wallow in a pool not made for thee. Rise up and wash. Thou wast proud and anxious to play. It is true that thou chose thy naïve knowledge over my wisdom and, indeed, became …"

"I became a shameful harlot dancing in the dung with a bunch of wild gypsies!"

She began to beat her breast and wail mournfully.

"Thou wast muddied from a murky pond and cajoled by maidens eager for some sport"

"I, myself, was wicked and supped on innocent, stolen flesh!" She sobbed outright.

"Indeed, quite a distance from the sharing of bright shods, methinks…" He paused to ponder. "Perhaps thou didst not know that the ways which seem right can be a maze to death."

"I have lost all taste for sharing…I've no wish for camaraderie." Her sobs began to lessen into silent shaking with deep gulps of sorrowful resolve.

"There is no wrong in seeking to share…the wrong was in…"

"…the filthy companions I chose." Gossamer wiped her dirt- smeared face with her greasy hands and began to cry anew.

Paracoeur sat silently, letting her weep her beater clean. He knew full well that her ears would not hear his heart until the plug of pride was scrubbed from them.

After what crawled like a Coeur d'Luz pass of time, he came again close by and lifted her sullen head in his giant, gentle hand. "Thou knowest that grime and filthy clothing are washable by clean ag. Come and bathe for I would speak my counsel to thine heart."

And she arose, with head still hanging. He led her to a quiet spring which bubbled, secluded within a bower of shrubs. Reaching into his poke, he retrieved a sponge sopped in vinegar and handed it to her.

"Scrub out thine ears, my lady." He instructed.

"Alas," she sighed largely "I can not scour the pictures from my mind or the heaviness of mine own soul. I have fair grieved thee and am unfit for the King's son." She pronounced, stepping timidly within the spring's bubbly border.

"I do not grieve for the living. And disappointment does not dwell within my being. I am charged by my King to deliver thee, spotless to thy betrothed. And yet I will. Hold thy shield with that vert, my lady ....And do not forget to scrub thy lips, they drip with rancid lard. One who would swim in dung- fouled water will occasionally. ..."

"I fairly reek with stink; so much so that half my tears fled my eyes for fear of it."

Paracoeur's eyebrow lifted arched over his luz- filled eye. "Indeed, it was not pleasant. Now, Little Maid, bathe whilst I scrub out thy garment and see to the repairs of thy garb. And then we will sup on spring ag and herbs and talk of vert. Rather I will talk and thou shalt listen.... Thou must be strengthened before we leave afoot."

* * *

Growing ever closer to their destination, Gossamer watched the crowned city seemingly grow before her eyes. Abruptly rising like a volcanic cone from the shrubbed basin, its granite base was skirted with fragrant, towering cedar sentries. The speckled grey mount was crowned with a turban- shaped dome that shone like bronze in the setting rays of the Coeur d'Luz.

"Come morrow, we will ascend the slope and enter into the crowned city." Paracoeur stated his voice alive with pleasure. "Let us strike camp in the cedars."

The walk had been long this Coeur d'Luz pass, but an hour or so of luz remained. "Paracoeur, mine limbs long for a noct's sleep in comfort. There is light enough and we walk a fair speed. Canst we not press on to the city, enton?"

"Nay, the gates are barred tightly against the dusk."

"They might open for thee, the King's Liege."

"Of a vert, they knowest of me...but not of thee.... I will pile fragrant cedar branches and cover them with my cloak. Thou shall not lack for satisfying sleep."

A slight sigh escaped her lips and she quickly covered her gape with her hand. She truly did not wish to challenge her patient rescuer's wisdom. As darkness tucked them in for the night they whispered of lessons learned and coming days.

"It was not in sharing or companion choice, Little Maid." Paracoeur instructed with kindness. "Fun and haughtiness are often playmates. Thy error was in plugging thy ears from my call ...and turning thine eyes from the way I pointed. A sure way of escape...."

"It is difficult," she whispered back "to desire to escape that which pleases one's self."

"Of a vert, danger oft masquerades as innocent amusement; like a spider lays a table for a guest."

"Methinks, Faithful Paracoeur, that I again erred in obedience to thy voice...Why was I deaf to thy calls? "

"Thou trusteth thine own eyes more than mine voice in thine ears. Eyes feasting full are often tempted. Knowledge does indeed puff up; but ....

"...the King delights in humility," she completed his statement with a weary voice. "How ever will I arrive at the King's castle, if I can not keep mine feet to the path which thou hast chosen?"

"Thou wilst, because I am. Thou needest no other hope. Now rest, I will stand guard."

After his words, she closed her gape; but thought long about the words they had shared. Once during the noct, she reached out to touch the glittering smoothness of her shield, which leaned against a cedar root. For comfort perhaps; she could not be sure why her fingertips sought the cool edge of the shield. Of a vert, she was surprised to find the shield grown larger and she opened her eyes to confirm what her fingertips disclosed. There in the moonlight streaming silver through the cedar branches, she saw her shield grown large as a platter. Her Guardian, bent over the fragile lambkin, nursed its wounds and fed it with milk that dripped from his own thumb. All was well, again; her beater held peace and she slept a deep, refreshing sleep.

* * *

The climb in the morning was rougher than she had imagined. The mount was steep and slick from Dawn's morning dew. The crowned city was not easily accessible, even though ancient hand carved steps spiraled to the citadel. The two of them reached the city gates before the Coeur d'Luz hung directly overhead solely because of their own strength and vigor. The steps ended abruptly beneath huge timbered doors of at least twelve hand spans in height. The strange carvings on the door were gilded and of a tongue Gossamer could not decipher.

"What does it state?" She queried her constant companion.

"It is an ancient, but not forgotten ruling: *To depart from vert is to die like a dog in the street.*"

"A strange greeting,' she pronounced. "And it is not much of a welcome."

"Nonetheless, thou hast need of the instruction which lies within. Thou lackest yet for a weapon." Paracoeur replied.

"Paracoeur, thou kenest I am bound for the courts, not the brawl of the streets or the battlefield. Why insist on such array?"

"Quiet, now. Thou must answer correctly when the summons comes." He brushed aside her protest and stepped forward to sound the gate gong. It sounded low and pure and reverberated within the step their shods stood upon. Paracoeur sat on the top step and motioned for her to do the same. After many briefs, there was a scratching on the door above them and a carved panel opened.

A low voice boomed out from it. "What seekest thou?"

Paracoeur rose, pulling Gossamer to her feet and whispered in her ear. "Knock upon the gate, maid."

And so she did. To her surprise, the huge gates swung inwardly and opened before her the view of a great brass plate inscribed with many markings.

Again, the voice boomed "Ask."

Again, Paracoeur bent to Gossamer's ear. And she spoke tremulously: "I would know vert and be known by it, by command of the King."

A great silence fell for a space of many breaths. Again, the voice boomed "Ask."

"I already asked," she replied impatiently and would continue, but was silenced by a warning look from Paracoeur.

"To know, one must ask." The low voice intoned: "Thou hast not because thou asketh not."

Gossamer turned a puzzled look towards her companion. He softly stated. "Do not let thy pride stop thine ears…hear what is said." He replied enigmatically.

Her eyes flashed with a blue lightening. "Open up thy gates. I must learn of the King's heart!" she yelled at the brass plate.

A great rumble shook the steps beneath their feet. Clanking and rattling commenced. Gossamer reached out to steady herself against stalwart Paracoeur. The vast brass plate began to shake and shudder. The gates trembled. And then there was a loud crash and a smoky blue cloud grew before the brass plate. At once, the cloud puff disappeared; as did the brass plate. Gossamer peered forward to see granite steps, coated with a paten of silver, which rose toward the city center. The whole beyond the threshold was awash with a golden hue.

"The question was required," the low voice offered, slightly peeved.

Gossamer looked about but could find no one speaking. Paracoeur took her hand and together they started to climb the inner steps with determination.

The steps were lined with carved, sealed doors. Looking above, Gossamer noted that the entire city was encompassed by the great dome. Gossamer saw enton that it was not crafted of metal, but of faceted sandmelt that reflected some of Coeur d' Luz's rays. It also allowed some light to filter through which in turn bathed the street with a golden tint. No one stirred about. The shods of Paracoeur and Gossamer scuffed against the silver paten steps producing a slight ring that echoed from the Dome's facets until a bright sterling melody accompanied their progress. Together, they reached the yawning door at the head of the steps.

Paracoeur rested his hand on hers and shared: "I have need to carry this wee lambkin to an infirmary. This citadel is renowned for instruction and marvelous surgeries. Thou must enter here of thine own accord. I will meet with thee soon."

Wanting to hesitate, Gossamer found herself emboldened by Paracoeur's touch and she stepped up onto the engraved silver ingot of ingress. The great arched room before her was filled with scrolls and many people; well-weathered men and women, with wreathed heads, who wore gowns that dusted the silver tiled floor. These gave no notice to the slender maiden who stood on the threshold. She felt quite alone, even though she was surrounded by many.

Of a sudden, the low voice of the gate announced formally "The Betrothed Gossamer from Nunatok!"

Without a word, many looked her over; straight-away, nodded a greeting and returned their attention to the scrolls held stretched in their hands. But, here and there, heads bent, casting furtive glances in her direction amidst an echo of murmured whispers.

From behind a towering shelf stashed with cracking scrolls, the Ancient Eremite stepped into her view and glided slowly across the room to confront her in his now familiar voice.

"Delayed, I see. Where is thy appointed guide?"

She answered with the hushed tones of a chastened child: "He has gone to ply for care of an injured lambkin. He bid me enter."

"So, he did…so, he did. A lambkin, ye say? Another casualty, no doubt …such carnage the trail holds!" He spoke low with vexation. "Come. Let us make the rounds…..many have groaned long to witness thine unveiling." The Eremite's eyes traveled over the young maiden and paused at a smudge of tarnish upon her breastplate. "Skillfully crafted, I see…and overdue a polish," He mumbled as he took her hand and led her forth into the maze of shelves and tables.

The great arched roof echoed even the slightest step or half roll of a scroll. Gossamer wrinkled her nost involuntarily in the stale, dust- hung air. She had bowed low and shaken so many wrinkled hands that she grew dizzy and befuddled; clearly quite unable to discern one hoary head from another. Now she sat, upon a cold seat of carved marble, before a table spread with but one scroll.

"Read." The Eremite urged. "Read and find that which thine heart seeks."

Being justly reticent in the presence of the Ancient Eremite, she bent her head obediently over the scroll of parchment and began to read. Her lips mouthed the words she had no voice for.

And she read. At first the markings appeared eccentric, like the view on a misty morning, and she could scarce draw significance from them. But she was greatly intrigued and peered more closely until her nost drank deeply of the parchment scent. She did not remember when the mist cleared. Only later would she remember that she had, without thought, reached again to finger the golden shield on her back. Little by little, like treacle courts an invalid's appetite, the markings became words. These became thoughts that became wondrous tales full of mystery and conflict which consumed her concentration much as a fire clamors for and devours wood. Until each new word did not satisfy; but rather fed, afresh, the fiery hunger in her soul that had been sparked as she stood outside the entry gates. The scroll seemed to leap to life before her very eyes; vibrantly breathing life into her. She did not notice when the golden hue of the room darkened; or when a mute hand offered a tallow candle to lend light. She did not notice the hour of sup that passed without a single protest from her rumbler. She was not aware of the dwindling echoes in the Great Arched room. She forgot the stale, dust hung air and breathed deeply of parchment and far away bazaars and fragrant myrrh. She did not long for sleep when deep shadows filled the room. She read. She fed her ravenous soul with beauty and awe.

Like a skilled weaver, her heart followed a single thread of scarlet through a colossal tapestry. The trail of a King and his sacrificial love traversed the scroll and walked into her very being. Although she had been pledged from before her birth and heard often of his name, it was now and only now that she began to behold her future groom. She became breathless with a blush that painted her whole. She became aware of his love, unequalled in all that is or all that was or all that ever shall be known. She was speechless and void of thought, but flooded with emotions that pulled her in every which way, much as the flooding ag beast had done. An extensive scope of sensation, too large to survey, swept her along and battered her against the canyons of human experience. Beyond comprehension, the sensations dwarfed her in their strength. There was no reasoning that could harness them. Before breakfast, she fell deeply and irrevocably in love with He, to whom she was pledged.

She felt the gong's vibrations through her shods, before she heard the low and pure peal sound thrice. Startled, as if from a trance, she was surprised to find the Great Arched Room abandoned, except for herself and the Ancient Eremite, who stood before her with a tray.

"Dawn calls us, Fair Maiden." The Eremite smiled a new smile that seemed not to fit the wrinkles in his face and that tugged familiarly at her memory. "I have brought a simple feast to greet her with."

Flushed at his obvious delight in her, she bent her head. "I am not worthy."

"Art thou judge, that thou assigneth value?" He replied quietly.

"Thou knowest of a vert, I am not worthy" She looked up and stared deeply into his eyes; unafraid of what she might find there.

"Eat, enton. Thyr strength is of great importance." The Eremite diverted her attention to the tray that he held.

Deftly he rolled up the massive scroll with the touch of his right finger and placed it under his sleeved arm. He spread a sparkling white-woven cloth upon the table and proceeded to place upon it a simple morning repast of clotted milk in an earthen bowl and the same pot of honey that she had tasted of the first night of her long journey. A pure white wafer of finest flour and a vessel of sandmelt filled with a deep ruby nectar completed the meal.

The Eremite looked deeply into the Gossamer's eyes and then took up the wafer, breaking it neatly in half. "Eat, my child. I will share this meal with thee. Dawn is more than pleased with this day and I desire thy company."

The Gossamer took the wafer from his aged hand and put it to her lips, but paused…a questioning look shyly entered her eyes.

"Nay, Young Maiden. It is beyond thy grasp. Simply share this meal with me. Thou hast been overwhelmed with our King, I see. Thou wilst require rest. Listen, thy friends, the stars, are singing greeting to the Dawn."

In silence, Gossamer and The Eremite broke the noct's fast. The velvet, cloying honey melted sweet on her tongue but awakened her with a bitter protest that was soon calmed with the comfort of the clotted milk. The ruby juice bitter to the tongue spilled a healthful sweetness throughout her being. The star symphony became a lullaby for the Gossamer who laid her head upon the Eremite's bosom, desiring the comfort of human touch.

When next she awoke, the shadows were long in the room where she lay. With a gentle glance, Paracoeur greeted her return from the land of sleep and helped her to her feet.

"The time is upon us to ajourney, my Lady."

"Oh," Gossamer vainly tried to shake the pleasant grog that clouded her mind and she nodded toward the lambkin that struggled to free itself from the Old Knight's embrace. "How is thy pet, the lambkin? Well mended, I hope?"

"Aye, and frisky, no less....but the lambkin remains here, this is not his journey. I shall return anon" Paracoeur was gone more quickly than it took for Gossamer to rub the sleep crust from her eyes.

"Fair Maiden," The Eremite stepped into her view, bowing low before her the sight of this act imparted great unease to her soul. "A boon has been waiting for thee, here in the crowned city." He stretched forth his hand toward her, holding what appeared to be the tightly rolled parchment.

When she, after meek protest, reached to take it, she noticed the scroll was wound tightly round a golden hilt of fine smithwork. As she took hold of the parchment bundle, the Eremite vanished.

"Grasp the hilt." Paracoeur instructed as he walked to her side.

Grasping the hilt, the Gossamer gasped in surprise when the parchment unfurled and disappeared with a snap. At once, she held in her hand a lionheart sword of seven hand spans length. With a highly polished cross-guard and a brass pommel, it had a fully tempered, double edged blade that flashed azure in the light.

"Careful, My Lady, where thou directeth that blade" admonished Paracoeur with a chuckle as he ducked out of harm's way. "That self-same blade will wreak havoc as well as protect."

'But, Liege, I am not skilled in its use." She stammered, stunned to hold such a weapon in her hand.

"Like any tool, its use improves with practice. Hone it with care. Thou wilst get the kenning of it, no doubt." Paracoeur reached out and placed his hand upon the sword's hilt. "I will guide thee in its use, but take care. It is a well forged weapon, not a trifling to decorate a belt." With a quick snap of his powerful wrist the sword became again a tightly rolled parchment. And he stuck the hilted parchment at the maiden's side through her belt, of a vert, finely wrought of three woven metals.

Befuddled with amazement, she stood in full array. Her garb reflected the golden hue of the great sandmelt dome.

"From here, my charge, we journey through the traitor's conurbation. But be not afeared." Paracoeur smiled encouragingly at her. "Nearer to the King's Courts we draw daily. I've mine heart warmed by the thought of sitting in his presence, a great feast in warm fellowship." He spoke, while rubbing his great scarred hands with zest.

For her part, she had not days enough to sort out her experience at the crowned city, let alone to understand Paracoeur's portent. But she spent this and many other Coeur d'Luz pass storing up in her heart a ponder to treasure.

SEVEN

purple cord

Stumbling, her nost deep in the parchment scroll, she would have sprawled in the deeply rutted road, sullying her woven cloak in the puddles that had gathered in the hardened ruts. As always, however, Paracoeur steadied her, catching her mid- fall and setting her upright again.

"Oh, My Liege, methinks I totter more now than when thou first met me ameadow." She exclaimed, glancing a brief up from her reading.

"Methinks thou hast grown a scroll on thine nost!"

"What?" Gossamer asked, lifting her head from the scroll, once more. "O, thou jesteth with me. I am sorry to be so engaged in the scroll. But, then again, I am quite serious about it. Thou kennest, it is how I can ken of my beloved. Why, how did I ever breathe without this scroll?"

"There are other ways to know of thy Beloved." Paracoeur stated mildly. "For instance, thou canst fellowship with those who ken him; myself, I have kenned him from the beginning. I have searched the very beater of him."

"Of a vert, Paracoeur; but it is not the same. Here in this scroll, I hold it. I read it. It comes alive to me. I decide which part to ponder. The other ways are second hand. I…."

"Thou fallest because thine nost is always in the scroll. What have we passed ajourney this Coeur d'Luz pass? I tender that thou didst not even glimpse the dance of Dawn this morning; nor the laborer who traveled by, wounded in yon wooden cart."

"There thou goest again, Dear and Faithful Liege! I tender that I prefer the scroll to thy mothering. "

"Prefer a dry and dusty parchment to a brave counselor such as myself?" He half heartedly bantered.

"Of a vert! See, I can close the scroll when I have had enough. But thou art ever…" She teased, demonstrating with a flourish and then continued on a more serious note. "Thou art too fine a warrior to hen about me. The road is wide and clearly marked. Dost thou have some peril to battle afar off? I hardly need an escort now. Why, thou kennest that the scroll contains a map."

"Ah" his voice lowered, "Thou wouldst have me forsake what I have foresworn because thou beginneth to decipher markings?"

"Thou needest not get in a sulk. I ken thou hast taught me well. I ken thy faithfulness more than I ken mine own beater. But that is just it. Thou hast taught me exceedingly well. I have mine own sword. I have the map. And to tender vert, I've things to be about which I fear thou hast no knowledge of."

"Oh? His voice rose in pitch, just a little.

"Yes, womanly things …I am to be wed. Think thou that I should learn to bride from an ancient, though extraordinary, warrior? I can not be fragrant with sweat and the tin of armor when I meet my betrothed. I fancy, he would prefer a wife without warrior garb."

"Ah, I see, thou desireth to browse the marketplace for...ah, suitable finery?"

"My liege, kennest that I love and honor thee; but dost thou expect to stitch mine wedding garment? I am a full grown woman now and need to be ...well, I have no need for a nursemaid." Petulantly, she almost stomped her foot, but recovered before the childish manner escaped her.

Paracoeur ran his fingers through his long, silvered hair and stood scratching his bearded chin. "The ground is different here. One must really be aware: unless thou desires to swim in puddles; as was once thyr habit." Paracoeur poked good-naturedly

Gossamer's face alighted with a giggle. "Nay, I pray thee. I wilt walk with mine eyes open. Just let me be about mine own business and thou canst have time to tend to thine. Surely my company tireth thee by now and it is possible thou wouldst prefer to fellowship with stout men for awhile. See, draws near a gilt chariot for the hire. Perchance, if it travels to the city, I can ride there and when thine business is complete thou canst meet me to sup in the marketplace."

"My Lady," his eyes darkening, "This is not wise. Thou hast no knowledge of the city thou layeth plans for and...

"Nonsense!" she dismissed his caution, "this city reads on the scroll map."

"My lady, hast thou perused thy scroll in its entirety?"

"I can read, Paracoeur, but I am not swift as a chariot puller. What I've read, I could recite for thee this instant." She was waving to the driver of the chariot, who was reining in his pullers. "Be a friendly sort, and let me have mine own thought, just this once. Thou knowest, I have grown in mine reason and can fairly make mine own way into the city."

Paracoeur grew silent and watched as she hailed, climbed aboard the chariot and gave a cursory nod to the other passengers. It was what he had steeled himself against for so long. His heart would bleed soon, once again. Like a statue he stood and watched as the words of the scroll passed into flesh before him.

"Remember thou mine voice, Beloved of the King's Son. Hearken when I call to thee." He called as the chariot drove by him, splashing muddy water upon his shods. He added, to himself: "I fear the scroll hast plugged her ears. O King, grant grace and favor to she who wears thy cloak."

It wasn't by design that Gossamer did not look back at her companion. She was exhilarated with the speed of the chariot and loved the wind in her face. She noticed little. Not even the leer of the driver, who permitted his eyes to have their way with her. The pullers were magnificent steeds, glossy black though frothy spent from speed. Gossamer held with all her might to the chariot rail to keep from bouncing right out.

The chariot did not slow as it approached the black tarred city gates. The guards at the gate stepped out of the way without a protest and the chariot cornered the gate with a speed that caused it to tip on one wheel. Gossamer was breathless with the thrill of it and was a bit sorry when the chariot driver suddenly jerked the reins up tightly. The pullers reared up and then dropped dead in their reins. The puller jumped out of the gild chariot and kicked at the horses with a hoarse growl. Turning back he stuck his hand suddenly in the maiden's face. Gossamer rose and placed her hand in his, grateful for the courtesy. He pulled his sweaty hand away and spat directly on hers.

Aghast, she wiped her hand on the woven cloak and a knot of indignation began to rise in her throat." My dear sir…'

"I ain't dear to no one, Missy. Ye ride with a brute; ye pay a brute's price! Do ye see what ye've done to me pullers?" He wiped his sweaty palm across his swarthy forehead and spat again, this time on the puller 's carcass."

"Why," she began to stammer a protest.

"Ow do I kin what in blazes ye were in sech a hurry fer.?" Pay up , or..." The leer returned to his eyes: "Er, I'll have me a go of ye. Thar ain't much unspoiled meat abouts. Worth a might, I'l wager.' He spat again, this time on the hem of her white-woven cloak."

Gossamer was appalled at the brute's manner, although she could not rightly discern what he spoke. She hurried herself down from the gild chariot and boldly came eye to eye with the man. "How much?"

"Ye kin the wage, it's posted."

"Sir," she inwardly shuddered to address him as such, "I am a stranger here; I do not ken the posted wage. "

"Ye carry a scroll…kin ye not read of it?" He pointed to the scroll which was tucked in her belt.

Puzzled, she pulled out the scroll and began to unroll it thinking perchance the wage was listed on the map. Before she could bend her nost into the scroll, the brute grabbed it from her hand, unrolled it half a turn and pointed his dirty fingernail about half way down the script

"Are ye an idjiot? See, here. "*Death*" it sez. Now pay up! Mi pullers are dead and ye hev got to recompense. "

"Well, there must be some mistake. I did not kill thy pullers. Thy hands held the reins." She said, her voice growing warm as she jerked back the scroll from his grasp.

"Awh, point the blame on me, will ye?" he turned and began to bellow: "Guard! Guard!

There's a live one gots the steel to renege on a posted wage!"

"I've half a mind to cut thee quick with my scroll sword! How dare thee play a word game with me! It is thee who robbeth me!"

"Awh, the fine maid has a rough side, after all," he sneered and continued to bawl: "Guard!"

Gossamer grabbed the brute's elbow. "All right, what will it take to quit thy protest? I am blameless, but I see ye want to vex me, regardless."

The Brute stopped mid-bellow and cocked an eyebrow. "Well, whut have ye got for a poor bloke like me's got no pullers, now cuz uv yer blazin' hurry?" His greedy eyes traveled over the maiden. "Well, tell ye what. I'm a bighearted bloke; it's a fault, I kin. The steeds were old…I'll take that shield of yers." He paused to cipher in the air with his chub of a finger. "Yea, it's a steal, but it'll jest barely pay the cost of one spent puller."

"I should say not!" She was shocked at his impudence. "The shield is valued well beyond yer diseased nags."

"Look, maid, I'm not in a mood to haggle wid ye. How 'bout one of dem shods?"

She shook her head vigorously, remembering a desert night. "Nay, the shods are fit only for me."

"Thar's always the melt down." He spat directly on her brass shods.

"Absolutely not!" she firmly stated while lifting her gown out of his firing range.

"Awl right, then, we'll step down to the smithy and I'll take a piece of that shield. And I won't entertain another offer, it's more than fair; so's don't try me ire. The guards in this city are known to take a hefty cut themselves; if ye'd ruther, they settle the wage..."

Out of the corner of her eye, she saw the guards approaching, at a lethargic pace, their flint black armor causing those they passed to shield their eyes. "All right," She groaned, exasperated. "All right then, Kind Sir," rolling her eyes and lifting her skirts further from the grimy street. "Let's make quick of this misery."

Aggrieved, Gossamer watched as the smithy took a chisel to her boon shield. The brute driver, all the while, rubbed his hands together, as if before a feast. It was with melancholy that she noted the shield was the size of a handfruit when it was lifted from her back. All's well, she reasoned to herself: it might grow the missing part again.

Taking note that the cost for sojourners was dear in this city, she determined to be shrewd in her marketplace dealing and inquired her way to the bazaar stalls; putting the morning's skirmish beyond her thoughts. "After all," she said to herself, shrugging off the weight of it, "this is to be my test of independence. I'll not be such an easy mark next time."

Like a whirling dervish, the market place reeled around her; a great cataclysm of sound, smell and sight which threatened to whelm her at every step. The distasteful odor of rancid, frying grease overlaid with the heavy fragrance of patchouli, cloves and cinnamon; occasionally, the fresh baked aroma of loaves wafted through like a fresh breeze. Fettered, squawking birds hung from their talons, showering feathers in their frenzy into baskets of coiled, shedding serpents. Chunks of oozing, draining meat hung above pools of clotting blood, next to stalls spread with satins and piled with rich brocades. The market place was swarming with swarthy laborers and kohl-eyed, heavy bosomed women. Shrieking children ran at play hiding behind stalls and leaping over piles of squash which lay atop coarsely woven bags ripped and torn with barley, rice and oats spilling out where scrawny hens scratched fervently for their dinner, clucking in delight. A discordant chorus of rough and wheedling voices plied their wares offering the bargain of the age:

"Lookey, Lookey, the very best there is!"

"For ye, I'll sell at cost."

"How about a good time, to ferget yer troubles?"

"Ye deserve better, look here!"

"Make a deal!"

"I have children to feed, it costs nothing to look!"

With her beater increasing its hammer at every turn, Gossamer began to feel confused in the tumult. Discarded against the rough-hewn stall walls lay piles of broken shields and crushed shods that tumbled ignored into the muddy aisles and were kicked about by those who hurried elsewhere. A queer unease began to gnaw in her rumbler. She bent to retrieve a shield shard, a handful, and looked at it closely, being jostled and cursed at as she slowed the pace of those behind her.

"Out a the way, Miss…this ain't no place fer gawkers."

"Wages are death, but there's no telling when t'will be collected. Meanwhile, a bloke's got to make a way…and live a little" another spit out as he brushed by her.

"Git to bizness or begone," said another " thet's what I always say. Ye can make a month's sups, if ye don't tarry for the show."

"What?" She turned to question the heckler, but could choose no one from the stream of shoppers who even seemed to notice her. Her hand went of its own accord to the scroll hilt and she became aware of a growing heat within her. But a piece of red silk caught her eye and she reached out to finger its sleek sheen.

"Ye like? It's the finest, no doubt spun just for the likes of ye, Miss." A gangly, shabbily dressed youth of about twelve cycles peered up into the pale maiden's face. "It suits yer color well. It's spendy, no mind; but," He surveyed her with a broad, tooth-missing grin. "No doubt, ye have the means to purchase the best."

She blessed the boy with a tender smile, feeling a pang of pity for his wretched garb. "Nay, thank ye kindly; I am amarket for only the whitest of white goods, fit for a princess. But ye look a bit thinned. Perhaps ye've been so busy ye've forgotten to sup." And bathe, she thought to herself but her beater was tenderly moved on his behalf: ""I am ahungered, as well, but a stranger and disoriented in this marketplace. Be a good lad and go and fetch two loaves and a draught of cool spring water.

The grubby boy smiled even more broadly, but stood his ground in front of her, stretching out his palm upright before her.

She looked at him and replied. "Go along, please. I've no need of a salute. I am just a person like yer self; although, garbed in shine, I admit. "

Perplexed, he held his palm higher toward her face. She could see that his hands were knobby and roughened with broken blisters. No doubt he was a hard working child. "My son... No doubt ye feel faint...Here take mine hand and I will lead ye to the loaves." She smiled down at him and took his hand gently in her own smooth hand.

He shrugged his shoulders offhandedly and traveled along beside her, nodding and winking at the other scruffy children that they passed. These others fell like a conquered horde in line behind the kind-hearted maiden. Soon the motley troop of them was wide enough to cut a swath through the market crowd. The more daring children craned their necks, as they marched, to examine their own reflections in her breastplate. The wee ones clutched at her skirts with their filthy, unwashed hands and looked up at her with unfeigned adoration. She stooped and lifted the most small into her arms and wiped its streaming nost with the hem of the Gossamer's white-woven cloak. Gossamer was wordless at the number of threadbare half-sized who flocked to her. Each quite emaciated and dirty, sought to be closer to her. No doubt their rumblers ached for want of sup; and maybe more. The indignant knot returned to her throat and she became determined to track down the caretakers of these children and upbraid them with a lesson or two. Why even the peasant shepherdesses had kept their wooly creatures with more care.

She was relived to see the loaf ovens ahead. And, even more so, when she thought she spied a head of long silvered hair towering above the throng that was gathered before the piles of loaves. Looking again at the foundling in her arms, she firmly resolved that, after sup, their next stop would be an ag spring.

With her charges in tow she halted directly in front of a pile of warm, just baked barley loaves and smiled at the children. "There ye go, I knew we would find it. Eat up now!"

The children simply stood and stared at her, agape. Not one child reached for a loaf. Perhaps, they want me to try the loaf, she thought, and she reached for a fragrant loaf and broke it in half.

"Whoah, there, milady! A sample, I'll profer gladly, but a whole loaf? Be a good dear and pay up now." A tall, fat baker, wiped his hands on his floured apron and stepped forward. "Ye've quite a brood, here. I reckon, ye'll need a goodly amount. A shield's worth, at least, from the looks of it."

Gossamer popped the first warm bite of torn loaf into her mouth and laughed a playful giggle. "How great to find a mirth in this rushing town. Ye bake a good loaf, kind sir." She addressed the baker with amusement and turned to the children. "All right dears, eat up now. And remember the way here so ye can follow yer hunger here next time."

The fat baker stepped in front of Gossamer and grabbed her hand. "Not so fast, Milady, I see ye are a stranger here, so I won't call the guard. It is customary in this city to pay before thee sup. "

Gossamer was about to speak, when she thought she heard her name whispered, nearabouts, but she could see nothing in the whirr of the crowd. "Good sir, a jest is fun for all; but let it be enough these half sized are near starved and ye have piles to fill them."

"I am good-natured, it is true; not at expense to mine own pocket. I'd not last a day in this city if it were so. I do not jest. The loaf has a price." He removed his tall-brimmed bonnet and spoke most earnestly.

"Sir? I have traveled wide and have never heard of such a thing. Thou kennest the King doth feed all his subjects to the full, quite freely."

"I ken this not. In this city, loaves, and everything else, have cost. Would ye wish me to starve mine own to feed yers? This flour is of the finest ground, I bake with skill. It is my due to receive a price."

"The grain for said flour grows abundantly in the King's fields and is free to ye. It is wrong to charge for that which the King gives freely." She scolded, almost choking as the knot tightened in her throat. He seemed a decent sort, but obviously had been misled.

"Ye must be jesting. I pay dearly for this flour. And I have never seen the King abaking. As a matter of fact, I have never seen the King. Who has time to travel to his courts when one has so many mouths to feed and bills to pay? Now buy or leave!" He retorted strongly.

"Sir," she taking a firm grasp on her scroll hilt. "Ye malign the Good King's name. I will fare report thee to the guards myself. Guards! Quickly, this man would spread slander of our King and would defraud his subjects as well."

"Gossamer."

She cocked her head to listen, but saw the guards advancing and wished to pursue this matter to its rightful end. "Seize him! He is a thief and a scoundrel."

She pulled the hilt from her belt and with a snap of her wrist, unveiled the lionheart sword. The sword's stark gleam caused the crowd which had gathered to gasp and fall back. The half sized, who had thronged to her care, ran swiftly to duck inside the edges of the crowd. Other merchants began to leave their stalls untended and shadow the black- garbed Guards who marched more quickly toward the loaf ovens.

The baker began to tremble with outrage and cried aloud. "It is she who thieves; I am an honest man making an honest living. She ate of my bread and refuses to pay what is just!" He grabbed her sword hand in his portly clutch and began to shake her wildly. "Pay up now or I'll have the guards flog ye!" He shouted, his beefy face reddened in rage.

"Gossamer!"

She heard her name clearly, but was profoundly outraged at the baker's unfounded accusations: "How dare ye, Sir. Unhand me this instant! Ye are well beyond propriety and will, of a vert, pay dearly for accosting me and for disobedience to the King's ways. Ye seek to profit from the King's own generosity. Unhand me, I say! Ye are indeed a ruffian scoundrel." Swept away in a torrent of righteous anger, she reached out and ripped his poke from his belt, tore it open and emptied his pieces of silver on the ground.

The burly baker was startled and saw at once that the crowd began to dive for his silver which scattered about. He loosed her arm to grapple with those who scrambled to seize his silver. He pummeled the bedraggled lad, whose missing tooth grin disappeared with speed. Gossamer wasted no time and raised her sword high above her head.

Energized with a fierce sense of justice, she screamed; "It is written in the scroll, thou shalt not ..." but her words were drowned in a shrill howl from the baker as the sword bit into his wrist severing the fist which had held the lad by his throat.

The guards plunged into the thick of the crowd and began to swing their swords about with little regard for accusations and obvious glee at the chance for swashing. The crowd fell and rolled about in a tumble of arms and legs and swords. The other merchants tried to seize the fair maiden from behind; but had to duck when her wildly swinging sword threatened their heads. The air was filled with the shrill screams of frightened half-sizes and the howl of a crowd, rabid and foaming, as it struggled for dominance. Above all, the voice of the maid could be heard shouting: "It is written, Know ye not? It is written..."

And the name of the maiden, "Gossamer!" rode the tumult of wind which whipped through the mob

An ear- piercing brass horn cut through the deafening din. In an instant, all ceased their struggle and fled in myriad directions into the marketplace which swallowed up the melee; leaving only some crushed barley loaves scattered about. The Gossamer found herself swept along a marketplace aisle, as well , by the press of the surging swarm of shoppers. Still breathing heavily and shaking throughout, like a pane rattled by the howling wind, her head began to clear from the torrent which had overtaken her. Looking down at her trembling hand, she was shocked to find the lionheart sword quite bloodied. She, herself, was cut. A deep crimson seeped along the edge of her breastplate and began to stain her white-woven cloak. Going limp, she began to shudder, but the crowd pushed her along indifferently.

Less than a stride behind, a powerful warrior with hoary head, the hilt of his great sword gripped tightly in his right hand and a small child tucked under his left arm, hurried through the press of the crowd. His face was stricken. Had he been cut of lesser stone, those surrounding him would've thought they saw tears streaming down his face.

"An elegant lady like ye should find herself at home in my stall. " A gaunt, turbaned man, dressed in desert dweller garb, stepped directly in Gossamer's path. "I have the very best, brought from beyond…" he closely scrutinized her and continued. "Nunatook, carved cedar imported from Nunatook…and incense: fragrant of star-filled peak nights." Peering closer, he added: "and ancient scrolls containing wisdom from undisputed mystics." Bowing low, he entreated: "My Lady ye are not a common lass. An unescorted maiden will not fare well, here, I fear. Ye look drained and out of place in this boisterous bazaar. Step in and take rest in my pleasantly fragrant, quiet sanctuary. Ye will find all the finery that ye have been searching for…at a cost reminiscent of times gone by."

Startled, she did not resist when the man took the sword from her hand, wiped it clean and tucked it in his own belt. Laying his manicured hand on her shoulder, he guided her into his shop with nary a protest from her. The scent of patchouli hung heavy in the shop that was draped with thick brocades and filled with many treasures. Gossamer submitted to his light touch, being in a state of shock, and he deftly guided her to a magnificently carved ebony chair, which was piled with black velvet cushions. She was very near fainting, when he flourished a gild porcelain bowl steaming with spiced tea before her.

"Here, My lady, take a deep draught of this medicinal brew. Imported from the east, it is said to have restorative qualities." He said, holding it to her pale lips.

The first swallow burned her tongue and she jerked back in surprise. He placed his hand on the back of her helm saying "There, there, my lady, relax. Breathe deeply of the steam. Ye fair need a bit of refreshment, don't ye?"

The shop was warm and Gossamer felt very weak as she sat wringing her hands together. The turbaned man hovered over her, plying her with one exotic tidbit, after another; his honey-like voice trickling slowly over her with talk of weaves and fashion.

"Perhaps ye would be more comfortable without yer helm?" He spoke softly, while removing it from her head. "Here, we'll set it here at yer feet. Ye can reach it easily when ye take leave. Although, of a vert, my lady, ye will find that few dress in full array when they are about the city. Perhaps in yer distant land, dress is of another fashion." He lightly patted her hair in place. "My, what a delicate shade yer tresses have. A jade comb would look divine holding them back. Don't ye think? No wait, I have just the item, a lapis ornament arrived only this week. It would reflect the azure of yer eyes."

"Of course, yer shield is exquisitely crafted and will purchase all ye could desire. Regrettably it is missing a valuable wedge. I hope ye were treated fairly in its exchange." He added as he rummaged through a chest. "I understand ye are in need of a wedding trousseau. I have expert tailors….. and the finest fabrics available, imported from afar."

"What? Gossamer stirred from her daze "I am not interested, Sir, in parting with my shield." The heavy scent in the shop was causing her head to dizzy.

"Oh, I can see why, it is beautiful, even though marred. Sentimentally attached? Perhaps the gift of an ardent admirer, I can see that ye would have many.... Have ye another then?" He held a diaphanous scarlet weave next to her face.

She brushed the weave away and struggled slightly to sit upright, her head spinning.

"Another, what?"

"Why, a shield, of course."

"Two shields?" She questioned incredulously.

The turbaned shop keeper paused and looked at her curiously. "My lady, I assumed that ye would have another, since ye are unwilling to part with the one on yer back. Perhaps, ye need to send for it. This could be arranged."

"Whatever for?" said she, pressing her fingers against her eyes, trying to clear her dizzied vision.

"Well, for purchases, of course. It is the accepted currency in this city." He shook his turbaned head "My, my, what on earth do they use where ye come from?"

"I've not the slightest idea. I've never shopped before."

"Never?" his eyebrow arched. "Ah, well, we shall remedy that situation. How unfortunate. I had no idea Nunatook was such a provincial area. And ye being in such need of fresh clothing; yerr garment is clearly ruined."

"Nonetheless, sir, I think I should be going. I have no extra shield and no desire to spend this boon. I am uneasy with the fashion of currency in this city." She attempted to rise. "Yer kindness has been most appreciated. I will not forget to recommend thee when I arrive at the King's court to recommend…"

"Not so fast, Miss." flint-gloved hands seized her roughly. "Ye must come with us, by order of the Magistrate.

"I'm sorry. I don't understand." Gossamer stammered and began to struggle against the grip that held her shoulders tight. "Please unhand me, there must be some mistake!" She cried.

"There's no mistake. It is clearly written." A guard retorted.

"Come along, now! Refusing to buy and sell according to directions; wearing armor within city limits, causing detriment to vendors…. We've no need to account to ye. Quickly now, stop yer struggle or I warn ye it will go bad." Another guard commanded.

She ceased her struggle as a heat began to rise within her over the rough and cruel treatment she was receiving. With voice under firm control, she insisted: "Unhand me, this instant! Ken ye not that I am the betrothed of the King's Own Son?"

"So, I've heard…so, I've heard." His flint-glove struck her in the head sharply, knocking her off her feet.

Half-lifted, half-dragged from the shop, she turned to see a guard counting out silver into the turbaned merchant's palm. She tried to reach for her sword, but found it missing. Greatly afeared she began to scream: "Counselor! Paracoeur! Help, I .."

Of a sudden his giant calming hand was on her arm. "Peace, be still, little maid. Do not fear."

"Paracoeur? I am taken in a snare. Draw thy mighty sword. Help me, please."

"I am foresworn to endure …the battle is not mine to choose." He bowed his head. "I have never failed thee. Remember and take heart" Paracoeur said. And then the determined guards roughly shoved their young charge passed the seasoned warrior with their charge.

In seconds, the swarming marketplace closed the path made by the guards. The Ancient Warrior stopped and stood erect; hand pumping on the hilt of the great sword he wore. His bronze face cast in an awesomely fierce mold.

Gossamer was barely conscious as the guards jostled and rustled her about through the crowd; it seemed the fight had gone out of her. Entering a black granite building they dragged her through stark halls and down stairs until they came to a halt before an immense door of glossy, chipped obsidian. They clamped heavy, iron chains about her. The door opened greedily wide with a low scraping, rasp. And they flung her, like garbage to the heap, down wide, stone stairs. She struck hard and then tumbled down until a great darkness swallowed her from their view.

It was dark; deepest, starless dark. Briefs had dirged slowly by until they had stretched out for what seemed like eons. Alone, nearly consumed by the ache that gnawed at her bones, she strained to hear if her beater still kept time. For a time-long night she lay at the bottom of the wide stone stairs, face down in the soft dust that carpeted the hard stone floor cell.

And she wept.

The tears had fled from her body in wracking sobs. She remembered with shame, first one thing and then another: Her milky white cloak, shouldered to the tiles in the Eremite's cabin; her greasy lips during a night's dance upon the desert sand; a nost in a scroll, too occupied to gaze into the kind eyes of her loyal friend and counselor. Shocked, she remembered how her well-intentioned heart had wielded a bloodied blade…How she had fallen for the lure of an incense-laden trap of a merchant's tent in a city that twinkled like stars in the night. She wept until the well deep within her beater ran dry.

The ache in her beater far exceeded the pain that greedily supped at her ebbing strength. Had the first freshly moc'd step from the meadow's carpet been in vain? She had failed to prove worthy of being foresworn. Waiting for the death that she knew was more than just, she sighed out one, long, last breath….

Of a sudden, her ears perked at the low, scraping rasp, far above the wide, stone stairs and she gulped for yet another breath...And then she blinked for a bright light burst upon the shriveled sockets of her eyes and coaxed them to open. The same bright light covered the chill in her limbs like a hearth warmed white-woven cloak and rushed flowing into her frozen veins like storm swollen ag. Surprised by strength, she lifted her head and tried to see through the glare of light that now carpeted the stairs. Above, the glossy, chipped obsidian door cracked and fell into pieces, like gravel, before the bronze shods of Paracoeur. Huge, golden sword blazing in his left hand, he stretched out his right hand toward her and she tried to leap to her feet, but like a tethered, startled deer she could not.. .

blue cord

The sunless sky had so frightened the village poor that they had remained in their huts for a week. But the plague had ebbed from their huts and muscles, long wasted, enton ached to move. The villagers emerged from their huts like timid quail from the brush after a thunderstorm and the long empty village square began to fill with the sound of muffled greetings. By afternoon, the villagers had swept the paths between the huts clean of refuse and each was secretly marveling at their returning vigor. A cart, draped with white woven cloth and laden with barley loaves, dried fish and honey rumbled into the village square behind oxen with polished horns. Below the loaves were grain sacks stacked five deep and jugs of oil. Three ewes, with swollen udders and gamboling lambs followed closely behind the cart. Amid a chorus of gleeful shouts, an impromptu meal was spread on the square's benches. Upon discovery of an herb bale, a fire was set and soon nourishing tea was brewed and carried forth into the hovels and huts that remained darkened.

The council chamber door, peeling and grey, was pried open. The air within stank horribly but a whispered plea was heard from inside the hall and the brave villagers entered the council hall. The few elders still living were carried out and kindly laid in the warmth of the sunlit square. Enton, Anna was bustling from one to another, coaxing their appetites with barley loaves and tea from the cart's bounty.

"Come…." a child's voice shrilled through the square. "Come and see!" The young ragamuffin sped from hovel to hut, like a village watchman alerting of danger. But it was clear there was no danger about, as the lad's grin was broad enough to swallow his jaw. Some of the finer huts remained plague-silent; but soon most of the awakened village followed the lad toward the edge of the village.

The Harbinger, strengthened by Anna's nurturing, pushed and pulled his self to his plague-eaten feet. Cai, also laid in the square, oblivious to the sickly sweet scent of death that lingered on his tattered, once elegant robe; he lay sunning himself and absentmindedly brushing the barley crumbs from his once well-oiled beard.

Cai shook his bone thin finger in the direction of Harbinger and cautioned "Take care …save thy strength and let the villagers run where they may. We shall have our share of work in days to come….look how the council door needs refinishing. Take a note…" Cai turned to the young scribe that lay stretched and pale next to him and continued… "We must raise a tariff to repair the council doors...they are an embarrassment!" Cai motioned to the elderly Anna, "Be a good woman and gather up the loaves that remain in the cart. We will store them within the council chambers ...No," he snapped his fingers as if to clear the fog from his thoughts "wait! Better yet …take the loaves to my dwelling and give them to my servants, they will ken how best to preserve the loaves for safekeeping. Oh, and send two loaves and a ewe round to the house of my old friend, Nico. I have not seen him in many a sunpass, perhaps he languors there in plague still."

Anna looked straight into the Cai's eyes which caused him to shrink back slightly. "I will gladly attend to the loaves when all have eaten their fill, Sir." She shook the barley crumbs from her apron and turned to follow the parade of villagers who followed close at the heels of the lad with the message.

The Harbinger, likewise, shook off the words of Cai and instead turned and followed the crowd, hobbling to catch up to the villagers at roadside.

"Look!" The grinning lad pointed across the road and the entire crowd gasped. The field was white with ripened grain that undulated like a calm sea beneath the mid day sun. Simeon, though age worn, began to jig his feet about in a dance of joy and was soon joined by many who sang and danced with delight. Never had any expected to be greeted by the sight of a harvest-ready field. There would be barley loaves next barebranch.

Harbinger gazed across the road and the dull film began to fade from his eyes and they widened with recognition; he bent his head and began to tremble uncontrollably.

"Come, morrow" Harbinger's voice was barely audible but he cleared its gravel and repeated more loudly. "Come morrow, who will meet me in yon field with sickle? "

"But, sir…thy feet are rag bound and thou hast scarce recovered thy gait." Someone in the village replied.

Yet another, timidly proffered "And thou art of the council…tis not fit for thy back to be bent in labor."

"Aye…tis true I hath been of council." Harbinger's voice grew stronger with every word. "I must bear that brand upon my heart, I fear, forever. I see before me, however, the labor of a kind stranger...I am not willing to let his labor perish in vain. Join me in the morrow afield and bring a sickle, if thou hast a spare for me. We owe a tariff from this field to the Good King, let us be prompt in honoring his decrees."

The peasants of the village paused and regarded Harbinger in one accord. As the pass of Coeur d'Luz grew tall, the grin of the messenger lad had proven more contagious than the plague had deigned to be.

red cord

The blood bead shattered the dreamless, trance she lay in, as it fell upon her frost-etched finger. It burned like dry ice. She would have jerked her hand away, if her body had not been shrunken beyond the strength to obey her thoughts.

Of a sudden, a melody joined the monotonous beat that had echoed throughout the dungeon. She willed her hearing to strain the melody from the air. She scarcely recognized the tune until, luz was hurled strongly against the darkness and the darkness fled without a moment's glance backward.

Her eyes were shocked blind by the brightness but just barely she heard the cooing of a familiar voice far above her on the steps:

"Oh, Good Prince! I have stumbled across the sight that my beater has always expected; but mine eyes shudder to see."

Her eyes widened and strained against the powerfully bright luz… Had she indeed heard the gravelly voice of her own counselor? She sought to find her voice while honey smooth lex dripped into her hearing, challenging the chant- like drone of the beads upon the stairs.

"Precious beyond lex thou art. Enton, I shall wrap thee in mine prized white-woven cloak. See even thy blood is swallowed within its purity."

With joy she beheld a glimpse of Paracoeur high above, upon the steps. Within his arms, he bore the fallen champion, wrapped within his own cloak. The obsidian door had been hacked from its hinges and Paracoeur was shadowed by the strong shine from Coeur d'Luz which poured past him and landed upon the slain warrior's great, golden sword. A great band of luz arched forward from the sword's blade and exploded within the dungeon with iridescent shine. From where she lay in the time-crumbled dust, the bone thin maiden could see the fallen warrior's stone-grey hand bloom with flesh color. Paracouer looked down the steps until his age-wise grey eyes met hers.

"Patience, Dear Maid…Just a brief and thou shalt also rise." He turned and began to carry the fallen warrior from the landing. Enton, as the shine from Coeur d'Luz embraced the dead limbs of the warrior, The Good Prince awoke as if from deep slumber. He left the embrace of the counselor and took to his own feet. He donned his abandoned armor and then lifted his great golden sword. The golden champion made haste down the dungeon steps to where she lay. With great arching swings, he deftly broke the iron chains that bound her.

"There is yet one thing remains." He spoke and then the golden champion ran up the dungeon steps, followed by the old knight, and their shadows vanished in the great luz that had devoured all the dungeon's darkness..

Outside, the city had changed. Smoke rose in great rumbler-wrenching reek, writhing wreaths around the obsidian city. The golden warrior slowly swept the expanse of the black city with his steel blue eyes. His gaze did not pause on the myriads of men and beast creatures that stumbled carousingly on the streets before him. These revelers seemed not to notice the enormous scaly form that lay, at its ease, where the marketplace had been.

The Dragon, its cold, blue-steel scaled tail whipping leisurely through the rock strewn streets, was swollen huge from its feast. It sat, picking its needle-teeth with a bone from a chariot puller. The dread dragon's teeth were stained with the blood of beast and man alike. Fire-red drool dribbled down its beard and joined with the bile that sluiced from its glazed, dagger-shaped eyes. Between its massive razor claws, shreds of fine damask and oriental silks were all that remained of the marketplace wares.

Sated, for the brief, by the carnage that littered every corner of the ruined city, the dragon's head lolled in a drunken stupor. Billowing, sulfurous clouds boiled in the sky above and the landscape beyond the broken city walls glowed ember red. Of a sudden, a magnificent luz shaft speared through the gritty storm toward the dungeon, sparking upon the golden armored knight and the faithful liege. All noise ceased save that of obsidian rubble crunching beneath golden shods. One eyelid rose up over the dragon's dagger eye, and it blinked from the brightness. Slowly the dragon laboriously raised its head, and began to swing in the direction of the sound.

"Thou art not the victor." The Golden knight challenged in a steady, calm voice.

Blue-steel, scaled tail grew taut and a quiver passed from its tip up the scaled hump between the dragon's spider gauzed wings. The dragon blinked again and then its eyes grew oval in surprise. A bone fell from its front claw and clattered upon what remained of the street. The vicious needle-teethed jaw dropped open; an insignificant puff of blanching smoke issued forth, but was inhaled quickly by a shuddering gasp. Surprise and shock washed over the dragon's features at the sight of the Champion and it spoke with a tremble: "Thou art invinccccible, wounded prinacccce," the serpent's voice grew in tenor and reclaimed its customary superciliousness. "Ahhhh, I sssssee we meet for the lassssst time. Welcome to my ccccity."

"Indeed!" The golden champion drew his great, golden sword and swung it in a wide arc above his helm. "Thou ken, O thou wretched Wyrm, that thy time has come to an end. Thy city tumbles into rubble around thee. For this is the Great King's appointed era. Scramble to thy claws, thou ineffectual, petrified terror and accept the justice of thy appointed obliteration. Bellow and quake thou toothless wonder, gorged to the brim with abortive arrogance." Enton, strode forth the champion directly toward the stumbling serpent beast that struggled to scramble back from the glorious, fiery golden sword.

Deep inside the dungeon, she felt the startling shriek that shook the stone cold floor and cracked the obsidian door in twain. She waited, holding her remaining breaths at bay, in stunned silence, until the brightness burned her eyes beyond their endurance and she allowed her eyes to turn instead to where her hand, enton blood splashed, had lain. She was amazed to see that the frost had retreated from her royal blue veins and an ever-pinkening flesh color was spreading from her finger tips across the shrunken knuckles of her hand, past her wrist and upward onto her arm. Before she could ponder the sight she heard the voice of her friend once more reach her straining ears:

"Arise, Little Miss, arise for I have come to thee like I once blood swore to do." The smooth-skinned, silver-bearded face of her beloved counselor hovered above her own face like a vision parting the mist in her mind. She felt her body rising, lifted gently by strong lithe arms that cradled her like a babe.

"Ah, such a sight thou hast, Little one…" Paracoeur smiled wistfully down upon her "Take thou no thought of wort, Dear Charge. See, I have retrieved thine white woven cloak from the smooth-tongued merchant," with his huge, battle scarred hands; the counselor warrior tucked the cloak around what remained of the maid. "Fear not, I will ferry thee to the Good King's Castle in mine own arms."

And the faithful friend and liege of the Good King turned and carried his charge up from the dungeon and into the Luz.

EIGHT

Light: cords woven tight

Wonderfully crystal-clear water cascaded into a bathing pool that was lined with iridescent mother of pearl and inset into the gold veined marbled floor. Although the spring was cold as the peak of Nunatok, the cascading water felt warm and healing to her bones;

as was the water's laughter when it playfully splashed the water lilies, which scented the water with a delicate fragrance. Gossamer had watched in a daze as the brawny, ancient warrior, Paracoeur had tested the stream of water upon his own, bronzed wrist, making sure it was of right temperature. She had sat still, perched on a gilt chair wholly aware of the mucked rags that clothed her and very grateful to have been asleep in Paracoeur's strong arms when they had arrived at the castle -------

On the last night of their journey, Gossamer had finally fallen asleep in her counselor's arms; after spending most of the night astonished and pondering while his bronze shods had made their way over the landscape, faster than the fleet chariot that had carried her to the obsidian city. Later, when Paracoeur had turned aside to speak in whispered address to the castle's attendants, Gossamer had scurried mouse-like through the doorway and into a passage beyond the room she had been carried into. With downcast eyes she had inquired her way through the labyrinth of halls until she reached the Great Cooking Hall, determined to become lost among the servants who labored there. Through the night as they had journeyed, a new strength had diffused into every part of her being and she had humbly determined to put her old ways behind and to serve with diligence within the walls of the castle that Paracoeur had insisted on carrying her to. While in the Great Cooking Hall, she had gladly spent some time sweeping the ashes from the hearth and pounding a pestle against many handfuls of plump barley grains. When Paracoeur had appeared once again at her side, she had been kneeling in front of an elderly maid servant. Her now slender, flesh-colored hands gently cupping the woman's callused foot as Gossamer washed the grime of the day from its sole.

"Come, Little Maid, it is high time thou bathed thyself spotless in the spring fed baths of the chambers prepared for thee. Come, leave thy service for a noct and be refreshed for the Dawn approaches and thou hast needs that must be attended to." He smiled gently down upon Gossamer's bowed head and reached out his hand to steady her rise.

"Nay, I wish to tarry here, Counselor. There is need for willing hands and I find myself willing." She sought his kind, gray eyes with her own. "Thou knowest well that this, if there be any, is mine rightful place within this castle's walls…or perhaps there is need for a swine maiden or ….Please…I am grateful beyond words to remain simply here….

Paracoeur shook his head and lightly grasped her averted chin with his hand "This is not the place prepared for thee. Come now and prepare to meet thy Good King."

"I can not meet him as I am not ready…"

"I quite agree." He chuckled. "I will draw a crystal bath for thee…and lay out a more suitable gown."

A tear fell down her ash -streaked cheek and she sighed deeply. "I can not." She began to shake "I can not. I am not worthy of such. Please give my grace to thy Lord and leave me to serve here…"

Lifting her face until his eyes met hers, he regarded her gravely. "Thou speaketh vert, of a sort…but that vert has lost its hold upon this kingdom. He, himself, has made a way for thee. Make haste." he pulled her to her bared feet. "The Good King waits godspeed for thyr presence in the Banquet Hall and the guests from far and near arrive. Think no more of times before….a new age is upon us."

Enton, the Gossamer sat within the crystalline bath. Its waters swirled around her like that bright and bubbling brook she and her counselor had strode beside long ago as they had traversed down the sides of Nunatok. Like the gifting of the king's white woven cloak, the water did not hold the filth that it scrubbed from her body. Of a sudden, the crystalline bath began to churn and its ice cold waters scoured her with force, like the ag flood had scoured the canyon walls with its unbridled force. Gossamer clung to the iridescent rim of the bath, sore afeared of being swept away. There was no need to fear, however, only the muck from the marketplace and all the filth from the dust- covered dungeon floor disappeared, just as if it had never been. The water remained clear and vibrant as fine, singing crystal. She felt the water's vigor soak in through her skin, the clear spring water chilled her blood until it stopped its flow and congealed into new flesh. The sparkling cold entered deep down into her bones and revitalized their structure, transforming the very nature of her bones .The water swaddled her beater with a new source of life. Gossamer was amazed at the water's power to cleanse and transform her.

"Hrrmph," Paracoeur cleared his throat from beyond the doorway. "Methinks, it is time, Princess, to make ready for the Wedding.

"What wedding? " Gossamer queried as she continued to lie with her head tilted back in the water, her flaxen hair streaming out behind her while she absentmindedly scrubbed behind her ears with the luffsponge

"What wedding? " Paracoeur cleared his throat again "Hrrmph! What wedding? What wedding, sayeth thou?" Gossamer could hear the Warrior-Counselor's bronze shods as he rose to his feet. "Why …thine own, of course!".

Barely hearing Paracoeur's answer above the bubbling bath water, Gossamer sat abruptly straight up causing the water to cascade down her back like a waterfall. She made haste to scrub inside her ears with the lufsponge, lest she had not heard correctly.

"Thou didst hear aright the first time!" Paracoeur shouted from the next room, making no effort to keep the chuckle out of his voice. "Aye, thy wedding be on this very day. "

"What?" Gossamer rose to her feet and grabbed the drying plush lying near the edge of the bathing pool "It can't be….I'm not ready"

"The Good King set this date long, long ago. If this is the day, than thou art ready"

"But...but," She stammered as she stepped from the bathing pool, wrapping herself tightly in the ample drying plush "I've nothing to wear...and my hair and...."

"Take peace and breath, Maid... thinketh thou the Good King a poorly host and father- in law? Of course, he hath provided thee with a gown and everything that thou needest.

For once, Gossamer did pause and breathe deeply, a sudden blush tinting her cheeks with brush strokes of palest rose. When she spoke, she spoke quietly and with great care. "Nay, Paracoeur, I ken that the King is good. Undoubtedly a generous host and wise Father in law, but methinks perhaps he doth not consider the right bride for his son."

"Thou kennest vert, that the Good King is wise , Gossamer....It is the Son's right to choose a bride and the King's good pleasure to confirm the union. There would be no better bride, as the son has pledged his love to thee. Paracoeur entered the room leading a parade of servants who were equipped with every manner of dressing device from tortoise shell brushes to shod latchets. "Here are thy ladies in waiting. They are skilled with the plaiting of hair but methinks the Prince would be pleased if thou kept it simply long and flowing. He has told me he is delighted with thee just as thou art. He loves the glimmer of gold in thine flaxen hair. "

"But, how could he say such things? I have never even met him. I certainly was no fair vision when carried within this castle last night." Gossamer shrugged her shoulders, lifted her arms towards the heavens and surrendered herself into the care of the attendants who guided her toward the wardrobe.

"So little thou hast learned to see without thine own eyes, my lambkin. He, the prince sees with his beater. I applaud his vision and his choice and I, methinks ye would agree, ken ye well, down to the very beater and marrow of thee." Paracoeur swung open the ivory doors of the cloisonné wardrobe to reveal but one gown within.

Gossamer gasped and her slender hand fluttered to her forehead. "It is…it is…I ken not the words…"

"It is exquisite, if I say so myself?" Paracoeur bowed deeply from his waist, flourishing his hand like a courtier.

"This is thiner workmanship? Oh, Paracoeur, why didst I hurry to that city to shop when the greatest of clothiers wast my true companion?" Gossamer lamented with a sigh.

"In part, young Miss…It is I who crafted it, but the son arranged for the weave of it and the Father ordained its design. Aye, and thy old friend, the Eremite, didst oversee the spinning."

Gossamer stood in awe before the wardrobe regarding a seamless gown of softly billowed, thickly woven satin. The weave glowed from within and was of an ivory hue. The gown was broidered from shoulders to hem, white on white with the symbols and story of the great Prince's exploits. The hem of the dress was etched in perfectly rounded pearls. The entire raiment reflected light by casting faint rainbows about the room.

Dewdrop shaped buttons of exquisitely carved jasper decorated the gracefully curving neckline. A lengthy train of pearly white roses was attached at the back of the dainty hourglass waist.

"I leave thee, Princess, to thy dressing. The hour long awaited by all the kingdom is nigh and thy Prince awaits his chosen Bride." Paracoeur bowed low and stepped out of the dressing room, leaving Gossamer in the capable hands of her ladies-in-waiting.

Later when Gossamer approached the elegantly carved door posts of the Good King's Throne room, her friend and counselor, Paracoeur awaited. He was armor-less, clad in a long sleeved, floor length tunic of seamless white woven with an edging threaded of silver. His silver gray hair flowed freely down his back and his beard was trimmed short and neat. On his head, he wore a circlet carved from a giant sapphire and engraved with the same script that was cast into his great sword. Paracoeur extended his arm to her and turned toward the magnificent room, that thronged with a multitude of people. Loudly in his clear but characteristically graveled voice he announced:

"Good King, Fair and Courageous Prince, ladies and gentlemen, ministering servants and eternal witnesses, I present to thee...The Son's Chosen Bride, promised by sacred bled- covenant, formerly of Nunatok, and soon to be wife and Queen at the side of our Lord and Heir King, co heir with him of the Good King's Kingdom: the pure and spotless Gossamer"

The entire gathering of beings within the throne room breathed a gasp, for the Bride was beyond beautiful and arrayed in much splendor in the ivory and seamless broidered gown. Before the Gossamer had stepped one of her crystalline, spun -rain slippers through the threshold, there was a rustling at the other end of the long room as the Bold Prince, resplendent in his golden armor, rose from his seat to honor his promised bride. He stood erect at the right side of the throne of his Father, the Good King, and watched as his bride who radiated humility and pure character walked down the marbled aisle towards him. The richly arrayed crowd parted before her like the fabled sea of red. The air was vibrating with the blaring of triumphant brass horns and harp strings that whispered like breeze-caressed wind chimes. When Gossamer had walked nearly the full length of the hall and was close enough to shyly regard the grey eyes of her groom from behind her lace veil, she gasped also. It was her Champion! The bold, golden-armored knight who had dared to face the horde upon the dungeon steps; he, whose very own spilled blood had dripped warm life back into her veins. Her lake- eyes opened wide and he smiled the smile that she had dreamt of since her time in the crowned city –the same smile that had melted her heart, forever. At the very moment in which that insight flashed through her soul, a majestic, rolling voice sounded from the Great Jasper Throne at the Prince's side:

"This is my daughter, in whom I am well pleased. Welcome Daughter Gossamer to the place prepared for thee before the foundation of this world. I rejoice over thee. Mine beater delights in thee. Who presenteth this bride for the hand of my worthy son?"

Paracoeur, stepped forward with Gossamer and took her hand in his own and placed it within the great grasp of the Good and Mighty King " It would be my pleasure to present this bride to thee, My King."

Gossamer was awed beyond kenning to find her slender hand in the grip of the Great and Radiant Light Being who sat upon the Jasper throne.

She bowed low and would have fainted if the Good King had not caught her eyes with the love warmth of his gaze. He clasped her hand safely within his own and spoke once more:

"Ah," the voice from the throne rose like the peals of the great bells of Zion: "My Liege and faithful friend, well done, Paracoeur, come and resume thy throne by me."

After Paracoeur had been seated at the King's left hand in the sculpted throne made of sapphire and silver, a great and expectant hush fell over the throne room. And then, the Good King tenderly placed the slender hand of Gossamer into the ungloved and scarred palm of the Prince. The King's unequaled voice broke the silence:

"Thine Bride, my son, I give her to thee. Rule, good as thou art, with her by thy side, for I have fashioned her to my liking as a helpmeet suitable to stand by thee. She is worth far more than rubies, my son; there has never been another like her in all the history of the world."

"Now let us advance to the banqueting hall, I have wished to celebrate the good fortune of all; for my Kingdom shall have no end."

"Yes, Father," The Prince's voice poured like honey through the air. "I have longed to sit and sup with friend and kin. The wine will flow once again, tonight. Firstly, I have wished to see my Bride's fair blush as I kiss her with the kiss I have longed to greet her with." Enton, the golden armored Prince removed his helm and placed it on the dais beside his ruby throne. He knelt before his timid bride, for he was taller by a third than she. He lifted the diaphanous lace that veiled her face with his strong, scarred hand, and bent forward to kiss the soft lips created for his pleasure. Gossamer felt verily drawn into the depths of his kind eyes and at once a flush of warmth raced through her being. On tiptoes she stood to meet his lips ....

When she awoke, she was being carried, cradled in the arms of her golden knight, through the banqueting hall. He peered down at her and with a musical voice cooed softly in her ear: "Ah, my dove...thou didst swoon...and I myself felt faint....thou art beyond beauty , my love......a gentle touch, I promise....A little wine ...a little bread will help thee rejoin the celebration , I believe..." He smiled at her and she felt more alive and whole than ever she had imagined possible; though, just his sweet breath that brushed against the lobe of her ear fair made her feel faint anew.

Upon reaching the head of the banqueting table, the Noble Prince placed her gently down into an ivory carved chair fit justly for her and then took his own seat next to her at the Good King's right hand. Beyond the Good King's satin beard of white light, Gossamer saw the familiar bronze face of Paracoeur, although for a moment, she had to blink her eyes when she thought she saw within his visage that like unto the Ancient Eremite's.

Before the royal family, the board was set as far as the eye could see, fair groaning with bounty from the four corners of the Good King's Kingdom. Chalices of newly pressed wine, herbs and pomegranates, tureens of whipped, treacle puddings, pewter saucers of mold pressed butters shaped like fleurs and tiny suns, steaming platters of brooklet shiners, baskets of dates and figs, ruby ripe cherries and soft, succulent peaches

Paracoeur tapped his chalice in stately manner and prepared to soundly toast the new joined couple when the great carved mahogany doors at the end of the banqueting hall opened with the tone of a warbler's birdsong. Those seated along both sides of the lengthy banqueting table ceased their talk and turned their heads towards the opened door.

In walked a host of village townspeople; their arms piled high with white and fragrant, freshly baked barley loaves. Their leader, wearing a rough rope-colored peasant robe and oil coifed hair stepped forth and bowed low:

"We request permission to deliver the tenth of the harvest, Good King."

"Permission granted, friend Harbinger" The Prince's voice rang clear and upon hearing the sound of his own name, the peasant leader lifted his head to behold a frightening sight. For a man strongly resembling the Stranger sat at the right hand of the Good King and called the Harbinger by his given name, "My Lord," Harbinger stammered and quickly bowed even lower.

"Harbinger," the Prince continued: "Enough of formality, thou hast missed my wedding....but art in time for the feast. Thou didst receive thy invitation in a timely manner, I trust"

The harbinger did not look up from where his nost nearly touched the embossed copper floor tiles. "Yes, my Lord...but I dared not come empty handed."

"Thou dost err in much generosity, Harbinger, and for this I call thee by a new name. Henceforth thou shalt be called Herald....because I see that thou hast brought a great harvest of villagers, as well as loaves. I, the Lord of the Harvest, am well pleased for thou hast become a good and faithful servant. Thou art always welcome here...come; take the seat I have saved for thee next to my old friend Nico.

As the very ashen-faced Herald rose to his feet, the Good King's voice rumbled through the hall. "Herald, thou hast come undressed for the banquet. Where is the woven white cloak that was sent thee?

"I am too ashamed to wear it, My Lord and King" Herald replied, bowing low to the embossed copper tiles once more.

"Embarrassed?" Paracoeur voiced from his throne. "What ever for? The cloak is of the highest styling."

The Bride, Gossamer, whispered an interjection on behalf of Herald. "It is not the cloak he is ashamed of, my Liege and Counselor, Thou kennest well. Why jest when the man is bent nearly in two to the ground?"

"I jest because it is preposterous to remember things of old at this of all times. Old things have passed away; all things have become new. Rise; Herald a new name begets a new being. Don thy cloak and join the celebration. There, the empty chair near Mary of the white weave cloak has been saved for thee. All of thy harvest have seat at the Good King's table. See, thy old friend Simeon is eating his fill for once."

A deep chuckle rose from the rumbler of Paracoeur and of a sudden the throng on both sides of the seemingly endless table was full of mirth and laughed a full while. The laughter was contagious and spread faster than fire eats grass. Soon, even the Good King himself was roaring a belly laugh that shook his whole light-being until sparks flew about the hall like fireflies.

Prince J' Desiree rose and unbuckled his golden etched breastplate and handed it to his armor bearer; who carried it away and placed it atop the memorial stone pillar in the courtyard. J' Desiree's robe was cerulean blue, like the first streaks which play across the sky when Dawn begins her dance. Around his shoulders he wore a cloak woven so white, that it appeared to shine. A circlet of purest gold sculpted to resemble the briars of the field sat on his brow. He turned his smiling grey eyes towards his Gossamer and clearly winked a blush upon her that spread from her toes to the tip of her dainty nost. Raising his impressive chalice he began to speak in his honey toned voice to the myriad of white cloaked guests.

"How I have longed for this moment when I might share of the fruit of the vine with each of thee, once more. Now, my long awaited Bride is content to stay by my side forever and I have need to thank both Maker and Keeper of the covenant." Prince J' Desiree turned toward the great jasper throne and his voice rose like the crest of an ocean wave:

"Good King and Eternal Father, I thank thee for thy Kingdom and for my Bride with whom I am overjoyed." Then the Prince called to Paracoeur: "Wise Counselor, Seasoned and trusted Liege, Everlasting Eremite, Thou art truly the road by which mine Bride has traveled to mine side. For time and time again, the story of thy bold deeds shall be told. Never shall cease the song of *The Princess and her Defender.*"

And with that, the Good and Highly exalted Prince J' Desiree raised his chalice high in toast of Paracoeur. Long and deep did he drink of the new wine from the alabaster chalice - that which was also a gift from his father the Good King.

From that moment on, nary a drop was spilt from the cup.

Dear Reader,

Thank you for investing your time to read this book. We hope that it proved to be an enjoyable and uplifting experience. We welcome your comments. These can be sent to weavestarproductions@yahoo.com Additional copies, should you desire them, can be ordered through the same address or from our storefront at http://www.lulu.com/weavestar.

Thanks Again and Good Reading!

Weave Star Productions*

P.S. If you enjoyed this book, perhaps you would enjoy others in our catalogue:

A Submarine Adventure,

A choose- your- own adventure book by Maggie DiRenzio and Jacob Dean, is a rollicking, breathless adventure taken by you and some colleagues as a reward for winning best-of-show in your science fairs. What happens next is up to you!

Expressions of the Heart by Joshua Hinckley

A collection of stories, essays and biographical sketches written by a courageous, overcoming teen who has determined not to let a life altering accident and subsequent brain damage keep him from his dreams.

In the Midst of the Forest...a tree
by Donna Luers Webster

An illustrated allegorical fantasy favorite of children and adults alike… all in the forest has fallen to the Dread and Awful Night King except for the flock that has taken refuge in a small, olive tree. There is a life to *In the Midst of the Forest*…a very present warmth at the gates of the heart.

The Princess and Her Defender by Donna Luers Webster

A blood-sworn princess bidden ajourney to the Great King's citadel, is aided in her astonishing quest by Paracoeur, an ancient warrior, whose fealty is sure and whose very existence is a paradigm of mystery. Set in a medieval kingdom, three strands: red, blue and purple- eternal truths braided together until warp and weft become woven strong in a tapestry of death, life and timeless love.

Coming soon:

Laugh with Me, Before I Cry! by Bethany Foote- Side-splitting funny and bittersweet journey into motherhood and the new life beyond. Available soon

Inteview with Jesus an illustrated book of Jesus' words. This is a book that celebrates the simplicity of paradox and the beauty of unveiled reality. Available soon

Children of God by Richard Webster - Drawn from the author's experience of working with troubled teens this book is an exploration of God's love for His children as seen through the heart of God revealed in scripture. In short, an exquisite tapestry of personal narrative, reality and hope. Available soon

Pre-orders welcome through weavestarproductions@yahoo.com

www.ingramcontent.com/pod-product-compliance
Lightning Source LLC
LaVergne TN
LVHW090944080826
845145LV00003B/887

* 9 7 8 0 6 1 5 1 6 5 5 4 7 *